The Accidental Summoning: Extended Edition

Addison Acres

Addison Acres

Edited by SJ Buckley

Cover Art by Addison Acres and SJ Buckley

Cover Photography from Canva Pro and Deposit Photos

Chapter Heading Artwork from Canva Pro

Print ISBN 978-1-923410-04-6
ASIN: B0CRKBDYW8
ASIN Print: B0CTV6R6K8

Contents

Acknowledgements

T hank you so much to my editor, Sam. I cry with every emotional support 'that' you remove, but I know it's for the best.

To my readers who take the time to leave reviews and recommend my books, I am forever grateful.

Content Warnings

P lease note that this work contains a relationship of a mature nature between two consenting men.

It also contains one incident of a forced kiss between one MC and a secondary character, plus threats of assault towards the MC.

Demonic Uber Eats

"Why did you summon me?" Zachariel demanded, glowering at the frazzled-looking young man who was standing in the dingy kitchen. It had been centuries since he'd last been summoned, and he'd honestly thought all the magic users strong enough to overrule Oberon's restraints had long died out. He wasn't exactly *opposed* to a summoning—it's not like he got out much anymore—it was just that he hadn't been expecting it. That tended to make him grumpier than normal and he'd ended up almost snarling at the poor guy. A kid, really. If he was older than twenty, Zach would kiss the Devil's rosy-cheeked ass.

Said kid was now flipping hurriedly through a well-worn notebook, his wide eyes darting up every now and then as if checking he wasn't hallucinating the demon standing in his kitchen. His floppy brown hair fell over his pale-blue eyes and freckled nose.

"Well?" Zach asked, arching one brow. He was trying to tone down how menacing he appeared but judging by the yelp that was audible all the way across the admittedly small room, he didn't succeed.

"I don't know!" the kid wailed, holding the book up and shaking it like he hoped something would fall out. "You were supposed to be chicken noodle soup!"

"Excuse me?" He surely didn't hear that correctly.

"I was just trying to make dinner," the kid said, utterly dejected now as he slumped down onto a chair at the table.

Curious, Zach strode over to the table and plucked the book from his hands. He flipped through it and grunted in surprise. "This is a book of spells," he announced.

"What?" The kid's head shot up from the table and he looked up at Zach in surprise. "My Aunt Harriett found it in my parents' things after they died. It was my grandmother's cookbook, so she gave it to me when I moved out here for university."

Zach noted way too late just how close he was standing to the kid, when he realised that from this angle, looking down on wide, liquid eyes and a pretty pink mouth . . . well, time to put *that* thought from his head before he embarrassed himself with a surprise hard on for the first time in centuries. "No, it's definitely a spell book. Cleverly disguised as a cookbook, I'll grant you, but there's no denying the power behind it."

"Are you saying Grammy was a *witch*?" the kid yelped.

Zach snorted. "*Grammy* is a ridiculous name to describe someone with such obviously strong magic."

The kid rolled his eyes. "Oh, my bad . . . Are you saying *Winifred Edith Phillips* was a witch?"

Unable to help but grin at the snark, Zach nodded. "Most assuredly."

There was a deep rumbling noise and the kid's face went red as he grasped at his stomach. He then grimaced. "Well, that's good to know and all but it doesn't really help with my dinner situation." He looked sadly at the pot of what was going to be soup—which was now sloshed over the stovetop—and then rather hopefully over at Zach. "I don't suppose you brought any food with you?"

Zach didn't think it was a very sophisticated look for a demon to have his jaw drop open like that, so he quickly shut his mouth. "Are you being serious right now? You get that I'm a demon, yeah?"

"Well, *now* I do, but you didn't exactly introduce yourself when you appeared in my kitchen."

"*You* summoned *me*!"

"Well, I didn't *mean* to! The least you could have done is bring me my chicken noodle soup!"

"*I am not Hell's version of Uber Eats!*" Zach thundered.

"How the heck does a demon know what Uber Eats is?" the kid snapped.

"We have the internet!" Zach snapped right back.

They both froze for a moment as the ridiculousness of their conversation became apparent, and then as one, they snorted with laughter. It had been a long, long time since Zach had laughed, and he'd forgotten how good it felt. The kid's stomach grumbled again and that set them off into another gale of laughter until they were both clutching at their stomachs.

"Ow, it hurts," the kid gasped between guffaws.

It took effort but Zach finally got his wits about him. "Okay, look—sorry, I don't know your name."

"Drew," the kid wheezed, finally calming down. "Drew Phillips."

"Right, well, Drew Phillips, you can call me Zach."

"Zach? What sort of a demonic name is that?"

It isn't, he thought, but didn't say it. "I doubt you could pronounce the name they have for me in the deepest pits of Hell," he offered vaguely instead. "Anyway, that's beside the point. Why don't we head out somewhere so you can get some food?"

Drew frowned, his cheeks tingeing pink once again. "Oh, well, you see, the thing is . . . I, um . . . the reason I was cooking . . . "

Zach looked around the tiny kitchen and his eyes were drawn to what appeared to be the rest of the apartment beyond the door— nothing more than a single room with a bed, a television, and a rickety free-standing cupboard. It was certainly not a luxurious space, and he realised that the reason why Drew was trying to cook was because he couldn't afford to eat out. He waved a hand magnanimously. "It's on me, of course."

Drew threw him a sceptical look. "What, you have Mastercard in Hell?"

"Don't be ridiculous," he scoffed. And then paused before adding, "We use Amex."

Drew snorted. "Of course you do." He then shrugged and averted his gaze, looking embarrassed. "I'm hungry enough that I'm not gonna turn down free food. Where do you wanna go?"

"I don't actually know where we are, so I have no idea what's available." Zach would never admit it, but he was eager to get outside and look around. He'd been trapped down below for so long now and he'd missed Earth. He hadn't been lying, they did have the internet—it was Hell, not a two-star hotel—but it was torture to see the world develop, to learn of the new technology, but not be able to play with it. To be forced to watch from afar. Demons who had returned from a summoning often brought back gadgets and toys with them, so it wasn't like he'd never experienced modern conveniences, but they weren't widespread. He was itching to discover things for himself, and he hoped Drew wouldn't discover the spell to send him back for a long time yet.

"We're in Nanaimo," Drew said. "Are you familiar with Vancouver Island, Canada?"

Zach nodded. The last time he'd been in Canada was well before it was even known as Canada, but he'd watched almost every season of every version of *The Amazing Race*, so he had a passing familiarity with the modern island.

"There's a little diner down the road," Drew told him, pushing back his chair and standing up. One of his feet caught on the leg of the chair and he stumbled a little, but he recovered and picked up the threadbare coat that was slung over the back of the second chair at the table. "They do awesome coffee there. Much better than Tim Horton's anyway."

Zach made a small, pained noise. "Oh, I haven't had coffee for ages."

"How long is ages?" Drew asked, pocketing his phone and keys.

"Oh, let's see . . . three hundred and four years, I think."

Drew raised a brow at that. "Man, the double-shot peppermint mocha is going to blow your mind."

"It sounds . . . interesting." He glanced up at the ceiling.

"What?" Drew asked, looking up as well.

"I'm just waiting for the lightning bolt to hit," Zach said. "I thought a Canadian not liking Tim Horton's was an automatic smiting offence."

Drew snorted. "Timmy's has its place, but you're offering to pay so I want something a little better than stale Timbits and lukewarm coffee. This place isn't a chain store but it has been run by the same family for generations. The food is good, the coffee is even better, and it might be more expensive than Timmy's but not by too much."

"Fair enough."

"Okay, let's go." Drew glanced around the tiny kitchen, double-checked the stove was off, and then led the way to the front door.

Zach watched him as he followed behind, admiring the juxtapositions that were Drew Phillips— lean angles and soft features, an innocent face and biting sarcasm, the body of a dancer and the grace of a baby dodo, the power radiating from him and the complete ignorance regarding its presence.

Yes, this summoning was going to be *delicious*.

Drew sat across the cream formica table from the demon as they waited for their order, a small frown tugging at the corner of his mouth.

Zach arched a brow at him. "Yes?"

Drew flushed a little at being caught staring but was secretly glad that he had—the eyebrow thing was damn sexy. In fact, *all* of Zach was sexy, and Drew wasn't exactly sure what to make of that. He'd never been what you'd call religious, but he also didn't live under a rock. He'd seen artistic depictions of demons, and none of them had ever looked like they'd just stepped off a catwalk. Looking at Zach there was no red skin, no horns, and no smell of brimstone. Instead, there were smoky eyes the colour of fine whiskey, an immaculate suit that clung to the demon's ass and thighs, and the spicy, alluring scent of expensive cologne. If he hadn't appeared suddenly in front of the stove, Drew would never have believed Zach wasn't human. A tall, dark, and extremely handsome human, but human nonetheless.

"I'm seriously beginning to think I have something on my face," Zach said as he turned to the window and peered at his faint reflection.

"Sorry, what?" Drew asked, finally surfacing.

Zach's lips twitched as he turned back to him, and Drew had a sudden, almost violent urge to lean in and lick him . . . to feel the scrape of Zach's stubble against his skin. He felt his face heat, hoping fervently that demons couldn't read minds, and he picked up the menu once more to hide his embarrassment. Drew had absolutely no idea where these urges were coming from and they were rather confronting. He'd been aware of attractive people in the past, but he'd never really felt any desire towards them, and he'd even suspected he might be ace, though the lust he felt surging through his veins at this very moment put that to doubt. Maybe the demon was doing something, messing with his mind? *Or,* a small voice at the back of his head piped up, *maybe he's just the hottest thing you've ever seen and you want him to fuck you five ways to Sunday.*

"Everything alright there, Drew?" Zach asked, the hint of a smirk tugging at his lips. "You seem a little . . . peaky."

He almost squeaked, turned it into a sort of choked cough, and cleared his throat. "No, um, I'm fine. I'm good, everything's good. It's totally fine."

God damn it, Zach was doing the eyebrow thing again. Surely he had to know what a formidable weapon it was? Drew scrambled to come up with something to say to distract them both from how pathetic he was being. "So, uh, witches and demons and stuff are totally a thing, huh?" Oh yeah, that sounded intelligent.

Zach just nodded, but his eyes crinkled in amusement. "Yep, we sure are."

Drew nodded along. "You learn something new every day. Are there other things, like werewolves and stuff?"

"There are people with transformative magic, but no, 'werewolves' are not a thing. The moon affects the tides, not someone's metaphysical state. I can't understand why people believe it would." His tone was the exact one Aunt Harriett used when she explained to their neighbour that she was never going to get rich from a pyramid scheme—a little bit condescending, a little bit exasperated, and a little bit fond.

"Oh, but demons with Wi-Fi are a thing," Drew snarked. "That's totally more believable than someone turning into a wolf during the full moon. What internet provider do you use? Do you even have an account?"

"We use Comcast and don't be ridiculous . . . we don't pay for an account."

"So you just steal people's bandwidth?"

Zach rolled his eyes. "No, we get it in exchange for providing lesser demons for their call centres."

Drew snorted. "Why am I not surprised?"

"It's a system which works surprisingly well."

"I'm sure."

"It benefits everyone."

"Except for the customers ringing in for tech support."

Zach sniffed delicately. "People who don't know the difference between an internet browser and a search engine don't deserve nice things."

"That's harsh," Drew teased.

Zach shrugged. "I'm a demon, what else do you expect?"

Drew leaned back in his chair to make room for the waitress who had arrived and was placing their food in front of them, the food which *Zach* had paid for after appearing in Drew's kitchen because of his failed chicken noodle soup disaster. He wanted to point out that he hadn't expected a demon to be so kind, or so intelligent or tech savvy, or to have such a great sense of humour, but he kept quiet, not sure if he wanted to push the boundaries and see what a demon was really capable of. All Drew really knew was that he knew nothing at all. It wasn't as if anything he'd studied in his MBA course had prepared him for such a situation.

Zach looked at the double-shot peppermint mocha in front of him suspiciously. He'd opted for coffee only while Drew got a proper meal. He picked it up and sniffed it and then his tongue darted out to lick at the whipped cream on top of it. Drew blushed as he watched Zach's cream-covered tongue disappear back into his mouth, leaving behind a smidgen of cream on his upper lip. He looked away just in time to avoid seeing that tongue peek out and lap it away. He hadn't had a chance to do his laundry yet and he didn't have any clean underwear, so if he ruined these ones by coming in his pants, he was screwed. "I'm beginning to suspect," Zach mused, eyes still glued to the beverage. "That this should be classified as dessert, not coffee."

"Well, it's a *mocha* so it's kinda both, rolled into one big cup of deliciousness," Drew defended it.

Zach took a sip, frowned thoughtfully, and then took another sip. "It's not *bad,*" he conceded. "But it's a little too sweet for me." He pushed it across the table to Drew. "You have it. I'll order some plain coffee instead."

"Thanks," Drew mumbled around a mouthful of the burger he'd ordered. He knew he was eating too fast, shovelling food into his mouth as quickly as he could as Zach signalled to the waitress, but he was too hungry to care. He'd been living on ramen and white bread, too proud to ask Aunt Harriett for money for food, and telling his friends that he'd eat when he got home to avoid spending money when they were out studying. It had been at least three days since his last proper meal—his best friend Todd went to uni up in Parksville and his family had Drew around once a month for dinner—and so all decorum had gone out the window. At least Zach didn't seem to be offended, doctoring the black coffee the waitress bought him with a little creamer and then savouring the taste as he sipped it slowly.

It took a matter of minutes for Drew to clear his plate of everything, even the salad garnish, and he drained an entire glass of water to fill in the gaps. He was feeling full for the first time in months, and he took a mouthful of the mocha, just enjoying the sweet taste in his mouth before he swallowed. It was the perfect end to his meal. "So, how long does this summoning thing last?" he asked, both curious and not wanting the comfortable silence to drag out until it became awkward.

"Until you send me back," Zach replied.

Drew bit his lip. "Um . . . how do I do that?"

"No idea," Zach said cheerfully. "I'm not the witch here."

"Neither am I!" Drew protested.

Shrugging, and looking totally unconcerned, Zach just said, "I guess you're stuck with me for a while then."

There were several problems Drew could see with that, the biggest being he wasn't sure how he'd survive being around someone as attractive as Zach without making an utter fool of himself. Also, how was he going to explain Zach to his friends? If they showed up and saw him, they were going to ask questions. They all knew he didn't know anyone like Zach, and they'd want to know where they met, who he was, and of course they'd be able to tell right away that Drew thought he was hot. Anyone who knew Drew knew he normally didn't react to an attractive person at all, so his bumbling and blushing would be like a beacon. He'd never live it down.

Before Drew had a chance to try and articulate any of this into a reasoned argument about *why* Zach couldn't stay around and that they'd need to find a way to send him home, Zach derailed his train of thought.

"Ooh, what's their pie like here? I haven't had really good pie in almost as long as the coffee."

"Oh, um, it's good. Really good."

"Hmmm, really good, huh? Really good as in, 'I feel like something sweet and it's better than McDonald's soft serve,' or really good as in, 'This is the best thing I've ever eaten before?'"

"Really good, as in I'd sell my soul to *you* for a piece," Drew said without really thinking, and then when it clicked what he'd said, his hand flew up to his mouth and he stared in horror at Zach.

Who simply laughed. "I'm a demon, not the Devil. My currency isn't souls. I am known to trade favours for pie, though, so if it's as good as you say it is, how 'bout I get us both a slice?"

Curious as to what favours he'd trade, Drew managed to nod. "Sure, um, thanks."

"What would you suggest? Cherry? Blueberry?"

He shook his head. "Nope, it's the banana cream pie for the win here."

Zach did his sexy eyebrow thing *again*, and Drew was starting to wonder if his eyebrows had a mind of their own. "Bold choice, Cotton. Let's see if it pays off."

That sent Drew spluttering but he couldn't find the words.

Zach laughed. A deep, rumbling sort of laugh that caused Drew's stomach to flutter. "Your face is so cute when it's shocked," he said. "After all you've learned about me tonight, are you still surprised I know movie references?"

"I haven't learned *that* much about you," Drew protested.

"But you've learned enough to know that my pop-culture knowledge shouldn't shock you." Zach's eyes seemed to twinkle as he regarded Drew. "*I* however am shocked that *you* got the reference. How old were you when *Dodgeball* was released?"

"That's not the point!" Drew protested, not wanting to admit the movie was actually older than he was and draw even more attention to his youth.

"I really think it is," Zach said, laughing again. He flagged down the waitress once more and ordered two slices of the pie, and she topped up his coffee while she was there. "So, you're at university, yes?" he asked.

"Yeah," Drew replied, nodding. "Vancouver Island University."

"What are you studying?"

"Masters of Business Administration."

Zach nodded as if he found this acceptable. "But no electives in witchcraft?"

"Strangely enough, VIU doesn't offer those," Drew drawled.

"And here I thought universities these days had standards," Zach said with mock disappointment.

"I'm so sorry to be the bearer of such terrible news."

Zach waved a hand magnanimously. "I won't hold it personally against you."

"You're too kind," Drew said.

"I'm really not," Zach replied with a wink. If Drew tried to wink at someone he either looked like a creep or like he had bad allergies, but as with everything else, Zach just looked suave and sexy doing it.

"So, do I really um . . . really need a . . . a *spell* to send you home?" Drew asked, suddenly serious. He toyed with his napkin, scrunching the corners up rhythmically.

"Yeah, you do," Zach said, and his mirth had dispersed as well. "And I was being honest when I said that I don't know what it is."

"Are you going to be mad if you're stuck here for a while? I mean, I'm sure it's uh, disrupted your day-to-day life just a bit."

Zach smiled at him and his heart lifted. "Trust me, kid, I'm happy to be here. Sure, it was a bit of a shock when you summoned me, which is why I was a little angry, but it'll be nice to be here on Earth for a while."

He sighed in relief. "Oh, good."

"Were you worried I'd be mad and would go on a rampage, torturing those closest to you and holding them hostage until you sent me back?"

He blushed *again*. "Erm . . . maybe?"

This sent Zach into a series of bellowing laughs that drew the attention of the handful of other customers in the diner. "Oh, that's just precious," he stuttered between laughs. "I didn't think I was that menacing!"

Drew's eyes narrowed—he didn't like being laughed at. "You're a *demon*," he hissed. "I'm sure you're good at acting all nice and friendly, but I don't think it's beyond the realms of possibility that you can do some really fucked-up things!"

Zach finally stopped laughing, and then he nodded. "Okay, yeah, you got me there. I *am* capable of some horrible things, *but* I don't have any intention of making your life a living hell while I'm here, Drew. I like you. Your friends and family are safe from me."

It shouldn't have made him feel all warm and fuzzy to hear that a freaking demon liked him, but it did. Drew tried to hide his pleased smile, but he could tell by Zach's expression he'd failed. The waitress arrived back with their pie and he watched as Zach dug in, holding off on taking a bite of his own. When the demon's eyes fluttered closed and he moaned a little around his forkful of pie, Drew hurriedly shovelled a bite into his own mouth to distract himself. That sound had shot straight to his cock and he was close to giving away how much Zach was affecting him. He may have Zach's promise that he wouldn't torture Drew's loved ones, but he seemed to be quite content to torture Drew. Slow, sexy torture.

Maybe he had hidden kinks he didn't know of, because to Drew, that actually didn't sound too bad.

Tether

They had gone back to Drew's tiny apartment and Zach walked inside like he owned the place, making himself right at home. Drew didn't seem to mind, just took off his jacket, plugged in his phone, and excused himself to go to the bathroom to start a load of laundry. Zach knew the kid had no idea about the limitations of a summoning, and so he figured he'd definitely have some fun with it tonight. He quickly stripped out of his suit, down to the snug, black boxer briefs he wore, and then waited idly by the bed.

The door to the bathroom opened and Drew stepped out, his pale-blue eyes going wide once more, this time at the sight of Zach almost naked—it was definitely Zach's favourite look on him. Drew's mouth opened, but all that came out was a squeak.

This was *so* much fun.

Plastering an innocent expression on his face, Zach gestured to the small bed. "So, which side do you prefer to sleep on?"

"*What?*" Drew managed to say, his voice cracking. His eyes were drawn down from Zach's face and seemed to settle on the softly glowing lavender gem embedded right above his heart, but he didn't look repulsed or even curious. If the dilation of his pupils was any indication, he was more aroused than anything.

"The bed," Zach repeated in a kind voice. "Which side do you want?"

"Why are you going to be sleeping in my bed?" Drew asked, his voice coming out a little stronger.

"Well, I'm certainly not sleeping on the floor," he declared with disdain.

"I mean, why are you staying here at all? Can't you get a hotel somewhere? There's not really enough room for you here!"

"Drew, think about tonight. What's the farthest we've been apart from one another?"

"I don't know! What does that have to do with anything?"

"Do me a favour, will you? Go out the front door and walk down the hallway towards the stairs."

"Why do *I* need to go?" Drew demanded. "Why can't you go? You have two feet and a heartbeat."

Zach gestured down at his current state of undress. Not that he cared of course, but he needed Drew to be the one to walk away, to experience what happened. The human need for decency would serve him well here.

And it did. Drew glanced back down at Zach's torso, his cheeks going pink, and then he dragged his eyes away and nodded. "Okay, yeah, fine. I'll go." He strode across the room, opened the door, and stepped outside into the hall. Before he'd gotten even a foot away from the door, he was yanked back into the room by an invisible hook, landing on his ass. "Ahhh! What the fuck?"

Zach crossed the room and shut the door, and then helped Drew to his feet. "You summoned me here, Drew. The spells for summoning always include a containment field, otherwise you'd have demons running off all over the place, *actually* torturing and murdering your loved ones. This one looks to be set to about ten feet."

His face paled as this sank in. "You mean . . ."

"Yes, I *literally* mean you're stuck with me."

"But . . . how am I going to explain that?" Drew cried, beginning to panic. "I have classes to attend! And study groups. And I have to visit Aunt Harriett at some stage!" He clutched at his head, fisting his hair and tugging on the strands as he paced back and forth. "What are we going to do? Shit, this is insane!"

As Drew swept past Zach again, he reached out and snagged him by the shoulders, bringing him to a halt and angling him so he was facing Zach. "Drew, calm down. I have some ideas, okay, but let's just wait until morning to go over them. I don't want you freaking out any more than you already are."

"Oh shit, oh shit, oh shit, you're going to do crazy things to my friends' memories, aren't you? You'll wipe their minds and they'll forget they ever saw you, or worse, they'll believe they don't know me at all. Oh, God, you can't do that to Aunt Harriett, please. She's given up so much for me as it is. Please don't hurt her, Zach, I'm begging you, please—"

Zach reached up and placed a hand on Drew's forehead. "Sleep," he murmured and then caught him as he slumped against Zach. He felt bad about forcing Drew into a sleep but he'd been almost hysterical and needed to calm down. A good night's rest was what he needed and he'd be calmer in the morning. Scooping Drew into his arms, Zach turned and placed him down on the bed and then climbed in next to him. He reached up and gently moved Drew's head so he wouldn't wake up with a crick in his neck, and then he concentrated briefly and the lights went out. The room wasn't dark, though. The gem in his chest produced a pale glow that illuminated the soft features of Drew's face, making him appear almost angelic. With an ache in his chest, Zach forced himself not to dwell on the past, and he finally fell asleep.

When Zach woke the next morning, Drew had migrated across the small distance that had been between them during the night and had wrapped himself around Zach. Well aware that Drew would probably pull away out of sheer embarrassment if he realised, Zach carefully began to extract himself. He was almost certain the kid was completely inexperienced, and as much as he thought Drew was cute—and was obviously attracted to him—Zach really wasn't enough of an asshole to deflower him. Who the hell wanted "fucked by a demon" on the record of their sexual history? Especially for their first time? No, it was better for everyone if Zach kept his hands to himself. Mostly. Maybe with the exception of some harmless flirting. After all, Zach wanted to have *fun* while he was here.

He stepped away from the bed and into the small bathroom to splash some water on his face, and even at this short a distance he could feel the tugging of the spell, like a hook around his spine. After drying his face, Zach pulled the washing out of the washer-dryer and neatly folded the clothes. He then went back into the bedroom, placed the laundry on the floor by the wardrobe, and sat on the edge of the bed. He reached out and brushed a feather-light caress to Drew's face, encouraging him to wake up, and with a fluttering of long lashes, Drew came awake and lay there, staring up at Zach, blinking slowly. "So . . . that wasn't some crazy-ass dream?" he eventually asked.

"Nope, it actually happened," Zach confirmed.

"I have a real live demon in my apartment?"

"I'm afraid so."

Drew nodded and lifted himself up onto one elbow, then reached out with his other hand to press gently against the pale-purple gem. "What's this?"

"Just some bling," Zach said, not wanting to go into his history with Oberon and his imprisonment.

"It's pretty," Drew murmured. He then seemed to wake up a little more and realise what he was doing as he yanked his hand back and turned away to scramble out of bed. He picked up his phone and illuminated the screen to check the clock, and then swore and hurried to the bathroom. "Crap, I have class in twenty minutes! I'm going to be late!"

Zach watched as Drew rushed around the tiny apartment, tripping over his feet as he shoved books into a backpack whilst simultaneously attempting to pull a pair of jeans on over the boxers he'd slept in. He watched as Drew then turned blindly to grab his phone and could see his shins were about to smack painfully against the bed frame. Without even thinking about it, he directed his magic towards the bed, sliding it across the room by two inches, just enough to prevent the collision. Completely unaware, Drew hefted his backpack onto his shoulder and then turned to face Zach.

"So, um, what are we going to tell people?"

"Tell people?" Zach asked, deliberately being an ass about it as he knew exactly what he'd meant.

Drew waved a hand between the two of them wildly. "About this . . . about you. Who are you? Why are you suddenly at university? Why are you hanging out with a loser like me when you're obviously super cool."

Zach's lip curled up into a smirk. "Super cool?"

Blushing, Drew looked away. "You know what I mean. No one will ever believe I'm friends with someone like you."

Once upon a time, Zach would have corrected Drew. He would have assured him he had worth, that he was someone people admired, but eons of having the goodness within him quashed had changed him. Instead, he shrugged and said, "Then perhaps we should avoid having any questions asked at all."

"How do you plan to—" Drew's mouth dropped open and his eyes went wide as Zach shifted into the shape of a brown and white cat before his eyes. Zach looked up at Drew, now towering above him, and wound his way between his legs. "What the fuck?" Drew uttered.

Now this *is super cool, don't you think?*

"Argh! What the fucking fuck? How are you doing that?"

Zach projected his chuckle into Drew's mind. *It's really rather simple. Instead of speaking out loud, I'm speaking directly into your mind. We're trying to avoid questions, not make people start asking them about a talking cat.*

Drew sat down heavily on the edge of the bed, breathing hard. "This is not happening," he whispered. "This *cannot* be happening."

It can and it is, Zach said. *Now come on, you're going to be late.* He nosed at the opening of the backpack, nudging the zipper open even further, and then he gracefully jumped inside, making himself as comfortable as possible on the pile of books.

Taking a deep breath, Drew got to his feet. "Right, okay, class. I have to get to class." He glanced down at Zach's head peeking out from the top of the backpack and then shook his head. "I'll deal later. I'm going to be late." And he hurried to the door.

Demon Pussy

Drew hadn't thought his situation could get any freakier, but the soft purr coming from his backpack said otherwise. He'd gone from thinking the world was a rather normal place to knowing that demons were real, magic was real, and not only was he now bound to a demon, but apparently magic ran in his family and he might have the ability too. He could barely concentrate as he sat in his lecture, his eyes constantly darting down to his backpack, then around to the people sitting near him when Zach began purring louder. What the hell was he doing? Was he *trying* to draw attention to himself?

The lecture finally ended and the noise of forty people getting to their feet and leaving the lecture hall deafened any noises Zach made. Drew slowly packed away his book, tucking it carefully to the side of the backpack so he didn't crush the demon, when he suddenly became aware of someone standing over him. He looked up and saw that it was Gwen, one of the girls who was in his study group. "Hi, Drew," she said brightly. Her long blonde hair was loose around her shoulders today, and she was wearing jeans and a VIU Mariners tee, looking every inch the stereotypical student.

"Um, hi, Gwen."

She looked between Drew and his backpack and said, "So, I couldn't help but notice some funny noises coming from your bag. Whatcha got in there?"

"Nothing! Nothing at all!" he cried.

"Uh-huh. Sure." Her hand darted down to grab his bag, and Drew lunged to stop her, but he wasn't fast enough. She dragged the backpack over to herself in triumph and went to open the zipper. "You know, I'm pretty sure it sounded like a cat."

Before Drew could reply, a white and brown paw shot out of the bag, claws extended, and took a swipe at Gwen. She shrieked and pulled away from the bag, sucking her finger into her mouth where a drop of blood was welling up from the scratch she'd received. "What the hell, Drew? Do you have some kind of demon kitty in there?"

Wanting to laugh hysterically, as that was *exactly* what he had in there, Drew bit his lip hard to contain it. "He's not good with people, okay, and you probably scared him by yanking my bag around." He opened the zipper and looked inside. Zach jumped out of the bag and into his arms and then turned to glare at Gwen.

"I didn't know you had a cat."

"I only got him yesterday," Drew explained. "He kind of followed me home. Didn't give me much choice if I'm honest." In his arms, Zach purred loudly and rubbed his face against Drew's chest.

"He's very cute," Gwen said. "I love the brown patches of fur. And these two tufts almost make it look like he has horns!" She reached out. "Can I pet him?"

Zach hissed and waved a claw threateningly at her. "Um, I think that's a no," Drew told her.

She lowered her hand. "Oh well, maybe another time, when he's more used to people." She tucked a lock of hair behind her ear. "So, uh, what are you up to now? Did you wanna maybe grab a coffee at Starbucks?"

"Oh, no, I think I'll give it a miss," Drew said, as he always did when anyone suggested they grab a coffee from somewhere on campus. He normally brought a thermos from home with instant coffee in it to get him through the day, but today he'd been in such a rush that he'd forgotten. As much as he'd love to get a coffee, he couldn't justify spending four dollars for a cup of overpriced coffee from the Starbucks on campus when that would get him enough pasta and sauce from the dollar store to feed him for a week.

"Oh, well, maybe next time," Gwen said.

"Yeah, maybe."

"I guess I'll see you later then. Bye, Drew."

"See ya." He watched her walk off, leaving him alone in the lecture hall. "What the hell, Zach?" he hissed once she was gone. "You almost took her finger off!"

Zach sniffed and began to wash his paw. *She had no right to try and look in your bag,* he said silently within Drew's mind.

"True, but it was still harsh. You made her bleed."

And yet you broke her heart.

"*What?* I did not!"

You certainly did. She asked you on a date and you declined.

"She asked me along to get a coffee, that's all. It wasn't a date!"

Zach sighed, a warm huff in his mind. *She was definitely asking you out, Drew. It's obvious she's interested in you.*

Drew frowned, then shook his head. "Whatever. I'm not interested in her, so it's a moot point."

Alright then.

Drew paused . . . Zach had almost sounded smug about that, but that couldn't be right, could it? He must simply be smug about the fact he'd gotten to torture Gwen with his sharp claws. That definitely sounded like something a demon would enjoy. It couldn't mean he was happy that Drew wasn't interested in her. That would be crazy.

Looking at his phone, he realised he needed to get a move on to make his next class on time. He held open the backpack so Zach could jump back in and then headed off across to the building where his next lecture was, stopping along the way to take a long drink of water from one of the drinking fountains and fill his water bottle. His stomach grumbled, empty since the meal Zach had bought for him last night, but he tried to ignore it. He would have to wait until he got home, so he drank deeply again, hoping a belly full of water would ease his hunger pains just a little.

After his lecture—in which Zach's purring caused several people to crowd around and coo over him—Drew headed to the library as everyone else headed off to get lunch. He knew keeping busy would distract him from feeling hungry, and he had several assignments he needed to work on. He found an empty table at the very back of the library, away from everyone else, where he pulled out his books and laptop and left the backpack open so Zach could get out if he needed to.

Are you not having any lunch? Zach asked as Drew got down to work.

"I'm not hungry," Drew murmured, the well-practised lie slipping easily from his lips.

You didn't have breakfast.

"Yes, I'm aware of that."

Then you must be hungry.

"I'm really not."

I think you're lying, Drew.

"Good for you. What are you going to do? Put me in the naughty corner?"

Don't be ridiculous. I'd much rather put you over my knee.

"Whatever, Zach. Can you please just drop it? I have work to do."

Drew could feel the demon watching him, but he ignored him and got on with his work. He had his pride, and so far he'd managed to hide from everyone how much he was struggling, so there was no way he was going to break down in front of a damn demon. Drew had gone days before with very little sustenance, and he'd survived just fine. Forgetting to eat breakfast and pack something for lunch was far from the worst he'd endured. He'd swallowed his pride enough last night when he'd allowed Zach to buy him dinner, but he wasn't going to make a habit of it.

Zach made his displeasure with Drew known for the rest of the day, ignoring him completely, hissing at him whenever he had to open his backpack, and one time even taking a swipe at his arm when he reached inside. It put Drew in a bad mood, and they were both furious when they finally got back to the apartment that evening and Zach transformed back into his humanoid self. "What the fuck is your problem?" Drew snapped, holding up his arm to display the three long scratches along his pale forearm.

"My problem?" Zach snarled. "*You're* my problem!"

"How do you figure that?"

"Because you're a stubborn child who refuses to take care of himself!"

"And why exactly do you think that's *your* problem?" Drew demanded, breathing hard, too angry to even argue about being called a child when he was only a few months shy of twenty.

"Because if you haven't noticed, I'm bound to you, you moron!" Zach shouted. "If you pass out from malnutrition, there's very little I can do about it unless there's something within ten feet to help you! What part of we're stuck with one another did you not understand? You need to take care of yourself, at least for my sake while I'm here, and that means eating during the day!"

"And what part of 'not everyone is rolling in money and can afford to eat at the overpriced university cafeteria' do *you* not understand?" Drew shouted back. He'd be lucky if his neighbours didn't complain about the noise.

Zach whipped his credit card out of his pocket and threw it down on the small table. "That was in your backpack the entire day. There's more than enough credit on it to buy a damn sandwich!"

"I don't need your charity or your pity!"

"Then what is it you need, Drew? Hmmm?" Zach stalked forward and with one sharp yank, he ripped the shirt off Drew's chest, leaving him exposed to the room.

Drew gulped as his nipples immediately tightened and his cock twitched. Zach ripping his shirt off was way hotter than it had any right to be, especially since he didn't have many shirts to spare. Dammit. He'd have to go to the thrift store to find another.

Zach's eyes gentled as he placed a hand against Drew's prominent ribs and sternum. "You're skin and bone, Drew, and you're on the verge of collapse. Please let me help you."

"Why?" Drew whispered, his voice close to breaking. "Why does a demon care about what happens to me?"

Zach looked conflicted, like he wanted to answer but he couldn't. He opened and closed his mouth several times and then finally managed to say, "I just do, okay."

"I don't understand," Drew confessed. "You seem to be invested in my health, saying that it's because you're bound to me, but then you don't seem at all interested in helping me find a way to send you back? It doesn't make sense, Zach."

"I'm a demon, kid. I'm not *supposed* to make sense."

Suddenly feeling dizzy and shaky, Drew slumped down into one of the chairs at the table. "This is all so confusing."

A warm hand landed on his shoulder, squeezing it gently. "I know. Now, can we please have dinner? You might not be hungry, but I'd really like something to eat. "

"What?" Drew gasped out. "Why didn't you say anything?"

"Because I didn't think your stubbornness would appreciate me guilting you into eating."

Drew let his head fall onto his arms, hiding his face. "I'm screwing this all up, aren't I?"

"We just have to figure out a way to cohabit for a while," Zach said. "I'm sure we'll come to some sort of arrangement."

Knowing he should bring up the issue of finding the spell to send Zach back, but holding back for some inexplicable reason, Drew simply nodded. "Would you like me to make some pasta for dinner?" he said as a peace offering.

"Sure, that sounds good," Zach agreed, his warm hand still lingering on Drew's shoulder. When he stood to go and find a new shirt so he could make a start on dinner and the hand fell away, a small part of him felt bereft.

Zach lay in bed that night, watching Drew under the soft purple glow of the gem. The salty tang of cheap pasta sauce lingered on his tongue and he wondered how on earth Drew had survived for as long as he had, living like this. Over the pasta dish that could only *just* be called edible, Zach had questioned Drew about his studies and his life, trying to learn more. He was studying under a scholarship, and one of the stipulations was that he had to devote himself entirely to his studies, which meant he wasn't allowed to work. The scholarship came with an allowance, but it only just covered the rent and bills and left very little for anything else. When Zach had questioned why he didn't live on campus, since it would be cheaper, Drew told him how it was a compromise he'd come to with his Aunt Hariett. She was a nurse and had seen too many university students in the Emergency Department for alcohol poisoning or drug overdoses, and she was terrified that if he lived in the student accommodation, he'd fall prey to the wrong crowd. She paid half his rent, but with the cost-of-living crisis, rent still took up most of Drew's allowance.

Zach had always been curious—some would call it nosy—and he'd prodded for more information about Drew's past. Apparently, he used to live in Edmonton, but he'd been orphaned at a young age thanks to an icy road and a drunk driver. Drew had been uprooted from everything he'd ever known to move across the country to live with his father's sister on the island, just out of Victoria. His aunt had welcomed him with open arms, but she wasn't well off and she'd struggled to keep a roof over their heads at times. Reading between the lines, Zach knew the scarce meals had begun long before Drew had moved to Nanaimo and started university.

Under the pale glow of the gem, the sharp contours of Drew's body cast deep shadows over his milky skin. His tousled light-brown hair fell across his face, highlighting his sunken cheeks. Despite his emaciation, he was beautiful, and Zach wondered how Drew was so oblivious to his own attractiveness. He'd been surprised when Zach pointed out that his friend was flirting with him, acting as if it was some anomaly. Zach had watched all day and had seen the lustful glances thrown Drew's way by students and faculty alike, to which Drew remained blind. He wondered if he'd also be blind to the flirty innuendo directed at him by Zach?

Reminding himself he'd vowed not to touch, Zach turned onto his back, forcing himself to look away from the tempting man beside him.

He rubbed a hand absently over the gem embedded above his heart, feeling the familiar ache there. Even after twelve hundred years, he was still not used to the weight of the gem holding him down as good as shackles. Bitterness flooded through him and he attempted to dismiss it, but it was hard to let it go. The betrayal he'd suffered had not only robbed him of his friends and family, but his very life. He'd once flown so high, only to find himself catapulted to the very depths of Hell. Not a day went by when he didn't long to be allowed to return to his home, but as long as he was chained to the gem, there was no escaping his fate.

At least this summoning allowed him to escape, if only for a little while. He was still surprised that Drew had had the strength to summon him, *by accident* of all things. Even some of the strongest magic users had failed in their attempts in the past, but this kid, with no training of his magical ability whatsoever, had done it whilst attempting to make soup. It was ludicrous, despite having its benefits. It made Zach begin to question what else Drew might be capable of. Could he possibly even be able to break the hold the gem had over Zach? Could he free Zach from his imprisonment?

No, it was too much to even hope for. Zach had fought and struggled for centuries before finally accepting his fate. His existence wasn't what it once was, but it was by no means as terrible as it could be. He'd finally come to terms with it, and to even contemplate escape, even as a passing thought, would make the disappointment that would occur when it never eventuated too crushing. Best to dismiss the notion before he allowed it to take hold.

Next to him, Drew mumbled in his sleep, a soft little sigh of unintelligible words, before rolling over and pressing his face against Zach's shoulder. Zach stilled for a moment before turning over onto his side and slipping an arm over Drew's waist, his resolve beginning to crumble. *Fuck it*, he thought. *I'm no angel, what do I have to prove? Why not enjoy myself while I have the chance?*

They were still tangled together when the first rays of the morning sun filtered through the window and woke Drew from sleep.

Stubborn versus Bossy

D rew gave a little wave as he entered Dominic's house, where the rest of the study group had already mostly gathered. Dom's parents were well off and paid his rent, so the house was large and well furnished, and after two failed sessions in the library, the group now met there exclusively. They didn't have to be quiet, they could eat their lunch in peace, and they wouldn't get kicked out at closing time. It worked well and they'd all grown quite comfortable there. The house was located near Westwood Lake, so it was a little further away than Drew would have liked, but he'd gotten the bus timetable memorised and the benefits of a private study area outweighed the inconvenience of public transport.

Before he sat down, Drew got Dom's attention. "Um, I'm not sure whether it's okay if I stay," he said and opened the zipper of his backpack to show off Zach's furry head.

"Oh, wow, you got a cat?" Dom said, standing up from his chair so he could see better. He was shorter than Drew, with wide shoulders and huge biceps. His hair was dark and slicked back neatly, and the warm brown skin of his cheeks was scattered with freckles. He was always dressed nicely, never in clothes from Walmart, but he wasn't ostentatious and flashy with his wealth.

Drew instinctively pulled back a little. "Yeah. He's not very good with people, though," he explained and held up his scratched forearm as a warning.

"Ouch," Dom said with a wince. "That looks painful."

"Yeah, it hurt like a bitch," Drew confirmed.

Sorry, came Zach's voice in his mind, and Drew wasn't sure if it was his imagination or not but Zach sounded contrite about it.

"So you're keeping the demon cat?" Gwen asked from her place on the sofa. She'd kicked her shoes off and her socked feet were curled up beneath her, her long blonde hair in a ponytail today.

"Why wouldn't I?"

"Because he's an asshole!"

"He's just a cat, Gwen. It's what cats do."

She rolled her eyes at him. "Whatever, dude. It's your skin on the line."

Zach jumped out of the backpack and hissed at Gwen, then turned around and wound his way through Drew's legs in a figure of eight, rubbing his cheek against his shins every now and then.

"Is it okay?" Drew asked Dom again. "If he's here?"

"Sure, I love cats," Dom assured him. "So, does he have a name?"

"Oh, I hadn't really thought about it yet," Drew admitted.

Why not just Zach? the demon asked silently.

Drew concentrated on sending his thoughts inward, hoping Zach would hear him, but they hadn't experimented yet to see whether he could. *And how will I explain if they ever meet you in person? I'll look like a nutter for naming my cat after you.*

It appeared to have worked as Zach chuckled, and it was annoyingly low and sexy. Getting an erection in the middle of his study group really wouldn't be appropriate, so Drew bit his lip hard, hoping the pain would distract him. *Maybe they'll just think you want me?*

Deciding it was safer not to respond to that at all, Drew said out loud to everyone else, "I've got a few ideas."

"Lucifer?" Gwen suggested.

Don't even think about it, Zach warned.

"How 'bout Rudolph?" Dom suggested, holding his fingers above his head and waggling them. "You know, 'cos it looks like he has horns or antlers."

Several other names were suggested, and Drew dismissed them all, having a stroke of inspiration of his own. "I think I'm going to call him Noodle."

Gwen frowned. "Why?"

"Because when I found him, I'd been trying to make chicken noodle soup."

I hate you.

No you don't, Drew said silently as he sat himself down in an armchair. *Otherwise you'd be trying much harder to get home.*

Zach didn't dispute this, but he did jump up into Drew's lap, circling several times before he sat down, ensuring he'd stood heavily on every sensitive part of Drew's anatomy before doing so. *Asshole,* Drew thought at him, wincing.

Zach purred smugly at him.

They settled down to work but were interrupted half an hour later by the arrival of Drew's least favourite person—his high-school bully, Edward Masters. When Drew had first started uni, he'd been crushed when he learned that Edward had also applied to VIU. Drew had honestly thought it wasn't prestigious enough for the spoiled rich boy and he'd head either to the States, Vancouver, or even Montreal for university. It turned out that Edward's mother had insisted he stay close to home, and so he'd agreed to stay on the island. Drew had hoped the campus would be busy enough that he'd manage to avoid him altogether, but unfortunately, Edward was doing his MBA as well, so they saw each other frequently. Any hopes of Edward maturing to the point where he didn't feel the need to belittle or tease Drew every five seconds had been dashed very early on, but at least the pushing and shoving had ceased. Drew did his best to ignore the jibes and snide remarks, but some days it still got him down.

"Hey, everyone," Edward said as he waltzed in like he owned the place. His auburn hair was cut in an expensive style, and every piece of clothing he was wearing had an expensive brand plastered across it. His hazel eyes fell on Drew and a mean grin lit up his face. "No one told me Phillips got a cat. What's it like, loser, to finally get some pussy? It's the only sort you'll ever get!"

Drew rolled his eyes. "Very funny, Edward. First-class humour."

"I know you want to finally pop your cherry, Phillips, but just remember, bestiality is a crime." Edward snorted at his own remark and then sat down on the couch, knocking one of Gwen's books to the ground as he did so and not bothering to pick it up. This earned him a glare as she retrieved it, but as usual, Edward ignored anything that wasn't someone fawning over him.

Who the fuck is this douche? Zach demanded.

No one. Just ignore him, Drew begged, hoping Zach wouldn't give any credence to the virgin comment. He was almost positive he was the only person in his class who hadn't had sex yet, and up until a week ago he hadn't been too bothered by it. Sex simply hadn't interested him. Now, however, he could feel his cheeks reddening and he felt ashamed of his innocence. From the hints and comments Zach had dropped, it was obvious he was a sexual being, and being a demon hadn't dampened his allure. He already thought Drew was naive, but this would only cause him to think even more poorly about him. Drew had been embarrassed enough as it was that morning when he'd woken up with a leg slung over Zach's hip and his morning wood sitting snug against a taut stomach. If Zach learned just how inexperienced he was, Drew was sure he wouldn't survive the humiliation.

Zach sat on Drew's lap, kneading his thighs and glaring across the room at Edward. Oblivious to the creature's displeasure, Edward launched into an embellished story about the older woman he'd picked up in a bar the night before. Drew, Dom, and Gwen ignored him, but the others in the group were drawn into the conversation and they got very little in the way of study done. By the time Edward finally took out his own book and started reading, it was almost time for them to head to their afternoon lecture.

Drew's stomach grumbled, and he fished out the PB&J sandwich he'd been sure to make before leaving that morning. Zach hadn't been overly impressed by his choice of lunch, but was at least happy Drew was planning to eat at all. When Drew broke off a little and held it out to Zach to try, the cat narrowed its eyes at him and looked away haughtily. *Suit yourself,* Drew said silently. He was beginning to understand that Zach didn't actually *need* to eat, he just did so because he enjoyed food. That was lucky because Drew knew he couldn't afford to buy cat food, and even if he could, he didn't think his demon would be impressed by a tin of Fancy Feast. Trying to explain why he was feeding his cat only the finest steak would be difficult, so it was fortuitous that eating was a choice and not a necessity for Zach.

Dom began to pack up his books and Drew brushed crumbs off his hands and followed suit. "Did you want a lift to campus?" Dom asked.

"Uh, sure. That would be great," Drew said with a smile.

"Cool. I'm gonna stop and grab a coffee on the way," Dom told everyone else. "Anyone want to join me?"

"Sure," Gwen agreed, and most of the others joined in.

Get one as well, Zach instructed. *A cup of joe isn't going to max out my credit card.*

I didn't know you had a limit on your card, Drew snarked back in his head.

Zach sighed audibly. *Don't be ridiculous, of course I don't. Which is even more reason for you to stop being a martyr and use my damn card!*

I can't decide if you're bossier when you're in your cat form or not.

Don't make me scratch you again.

You're enough of an asshole that you actually would make me bleed just to convince me to get a coffee, aren't you?

Do you even need an answer to that? Zach asked.

Drew didn't reply, just picked Zach up and shoved him bodily into the backpack. "Sure, I'll grab a coffee with you," he told the group.

"You been working the streets, Phillips?" Edward asked. "Got yourself a nice disposable income?"

"Yeah, your momma tips real well," Drew snapped at him.

Dom crowed and slapped Drew on the back. "Ha ha, nice comeback! Come on, we need to get a move on if we don't want to be late."

Drew shoved his way past Edward, enjoying the offended look on his face, and was in a buoyant mood the entire drive over to campus and then the short walk to the Starbucks near the library. He didn't even feel guilty as he ordered a large peppermint mocha and handed over Zach's credit card. Zach purred loudly at him from the bag, and Drew reached inside to scritch at the top of his head. A rough tongue darted out and licked at Drew's finger and he wondered how much of the animal form influenced Zach in this state. Was he aware he'd just licked Drew, and had chosen to do it? Or was it all instinct? The barista called his name, and at the first sip of his beverage the question faded from his mind as he got lost in his enjoyment.

When his final lecture for the day and also the week was over, Drew sighed in relief and headed home. He'd not gotten as much work done on his assignments as he'd wanted to at the study group, but it was enough that he'd have most of the weekend free. There were things he needed to research and people he needed to track down. He was going to be busy.

As soon as they entered his tiny apartment, Zach leapt from the backpack and transformed before Drew's eyes into his human-like form. He stretched—not unlike a cat— his back arching and pulling taut the crisp button-up that was tucked into his form-fitting tailored pants. Drew briefly hoped the shirt would pull free from its confines and ride up to show off some of the tan skin he knew was beneath, but it didn't. The stretch was soon over, and Zach was looking at him with a knowing smile on his lips.

Drew looked away quickly and cleared his throat. "So, I'll just reheat the leftover pasta for dinner and then—"

"No!" Zach announced and strode around until he was directly in front of Drew. "No, Drew. We are *not* eating that horrid stuff for a second night in a row."

Frowning, Drew glanced over into the small kitchen. "Oh, well, I'm not sure what else I have here but I'm sure I can find something to make. There's a little bread left. I was saving it for toast in the morning but I could make toast for dinner if you prefer? It's probably too stale now for sandwiches."

Zach sighed and pinched the bridge of his nose. "Or we could use my magical money card and *order in*. Doesn't Chinese sound good to you?"

His stomach rumbling just at the thought, Drew found his hunger was stronger than his pride and stubbornness, and he nodded. "Yeah, it does," he said softly. "Only if you're sure, though. I don't want to feel like I'm taking advantage of you."

Zach rolled his eyes and then stepped forward into Drew's space, crowding close. "Oh, I'm sure, sweetness," he practically purred. He leaned down until his breath was hot and sweet against Drew's ear, making him shiver. "Do you really, truly believe it's *me* who is being taken advantage of here?" He reached out and trailed a hand down Drew's cheek and over his throat, then danced it across a shoulder before stroking down . . . down . . . down Drew's back. "Do you worry I'll think you owe me?" he asked, voice low and husky. "Do you think I might demand that you pay me back somehow?"

Drew was achingly hard in his jeans and also slightly terrified. He swallowed loudly and managed a nod. "Maybe," he admitted.

"Oh, Drew," Zach growled, and his hand dipped down even further until it was just resting on the swell of his ass. "I can think of so many delicious ways I could take payment from you. So *many* ways. But . . ." He paused, his lips tickling Drew's ear. "I think *this* will be enough." And he dipped his hand into the pocket of Drew's jeans and snagged his phone. Then he stepped back, looking completely and utterly unaffected by their closeness, and swiped it open. "So, any recommendations for the best Chinese around?"

Knowing his mouth must be gaping open like a fish but quite unable to compose himself, Drew shook his head. "No, no, anything is fine. I uh, I have to use the bathroom." And he hurried across the room, into the bathroom, and quickly shut the door behind him, leaning against the cool wood and breathing hard.

He could almost swear he heard Zach chuckling, but he didn't care. Drew ripped open his jeans and shoved his hand down into his boxers, closing it around his cock and squeezing. He came immediately, spurting over his hand, biting his lip hard so as not to make a sound. Drew wasn't under any delusions that Zach didn't know exactly what he was doing, but as he shook and trembled through the aftershocks of his orgasm, he found he simply didn't care. He was just lucky he'd lasted until he had some relative privacy, since he'd been close, way too close, to coming in his pants untouched.

When he finally recovered enough to leave the bathroom with a measure of nonchalance, he found that Zach had placed an order for dinner and was laughing at something on Drew's phone. He quickly checked to make sure it wasn't anything private, but relaxed when he saw it was just a cat meme. Drew grabbed his laptop and booted it up, leaving Zach to entertain himself with the phone. He opened an incognito browser window—really not wanting this in his search history—and typed in "witches and wizards in Nanaimo," but he didn't get a lot of hits and so had to expand the search to Vancouver Island at large. A lot of what he found was historical information, and there were a lot of sites for Wiccan practitioners and then numerous dead ends that took him to new-age bookshops, but finally, on the third page of the search results, he found something that seemed promising. There was a knock at the door as dinner arrived, and Drew quickly scribbled down an address in Ladysmith so he could go and investigate tomorrow.

Looking at the numerous bags of takeout sitting on his tiny kitchen counter, Drew turned to Zach and his lips quirked into a smile. "Are we feeding the hordes of Hell as well? Should I have prepared for company?"

Zach sniffed as he pulled out several containers of rice. "I'm on vacation. Why would I want to invite my colleagues?"

Drew opened a container of honey pepper beef and breathed in deeply, salivating a little at the aroma. "Maybe to show off how you've turned me into a glutton?"

"Not my department. The whole sin thing is the big guy's job."

"Well, maybe you wanted me to meet the family," Drew teased as he fished a piece of beef out and popped it into his mouth.

Zach went still, and all amusement fell from his face. "I don't have any family in Hell," he said, voice tight with something Drew couldn't recognise.

"Zach, I—"

"Drew," the demon said, cutting him off. "Let's just eat, yeah?"

It was clear the discussion was over and Drew didn't push it, just got out two plates and handed one over before filling his own. Zach obviously didn't like talking about his life, and Drew respected that, though it made their—would he call it a friendship?—decidedly one-sided. Zach knew much more about Drew than Drew did about him, but he'd been raised to respect personal boundaries and he wasn't going to pry when it wasn't welcome. He could admit to himself, though, he was *very* curious about Zach's past. He just hoped that perhaps one day, before this was all over, he'd get some answers.

"Do you want to watch something?" Drew asked, gesturing behind him to the TV.

"Sure," Zach agreed easily enough, and Drew was relieved he wasn't still upset.

"Um, I don't have Netflix or anything, but I have some DVDs." He left the kitchen and went over to the small stack of discs next to the TV in the main room. He read out the titles, and Zach picked out the *Wrath of Khan*. They settled down on the bed to watch it, and as Zach's thigh pressed close against Drew's, he began to regret not having a couch. He could feel his cock growing hard again, just from being so close to Zach, and his earlier orgasm felt like it had been years ago. Drew sighed and tried to will it away, knowing he couldn't excuse himself again to go and jerk off in the bathroom. He refused to look over at Zach, worried the demon would *know* he was hard and that it was because of him. Drew couldn't stand to see the sexy smirk on his face, the knowing smile, the amused glint in his eyes. He'd embarrassed himself more than enough for one night.

Drew wasn't able to concentrate on the movie, too busy with his internal conflict as he fought his attraction to the demon. Eventually, he fell asleep, and when he woke the next morning with Zach wrapped around him, he began to question if he should even fight it anymore. There was no way to know how long Zach would be part of his life, and if he found the spell to reverse the summoning, would he regret not taking the chance while he'd had it? It was easy enough to consider, lying in the dark with the warm bulk of Zach at his back, but Drew knew once he was up and about for the day, faced with Zach's charm and handsomeness, it would feel much more unattainable. So he closed his eyes, let himself drift back to sleep, and enjoyed the brief moment as all he would ever get to have.

Off to See the Wizard

They stood on the sidewalk of First Avenue, looking up at the inconspicuous front door, and Drew checked his scribbled instructions once again to make sure he was at the right place. The house in front of them was completely unassuming. It was a neat, older home with white cladding, steps leading up to a covered porch, and a side entrance to what looked like a basement suite—not somewhere he'd expect to find a wizard. He glanced at the numbers on the gate, confirming they were definitely at the address he'd found online. Shrugging, he started to make his way up the paved path to the steps, but Zach grabbed his wrist, stopping him. "Are you going to tell me what we're doing here? I really don't like being unprepared."

Drew's eyes were glued to the large hand clasped around his wrist and an image of that same hand holding him down but in the bedroom flashed before his eyes. He shook his head, shaking away the welcome but untimely image, and tilted his head towards the completely inconspicuous house. "We're here to see a wizard," he said.

"Excuse me?" Zach actually looked shocked.

"According to Google, there's a wizard here who might be able to help me find the spell we need."

Was it his imagination or was that a flicker of hurt in Zach's eyes? "You *googled* a wizard?" Zach blustered.

"Well, yeah? I don't know any personally, so how else was I supposed to track someone down?"

Zach considered this and then shook his head. "Okay, you know what, that's fair. How do you know he's for real, though?"

"I don't," Drew conceded. "But I figured you'd be able to tell."

Zach regarded him steadily for a long moment and then finally nodded, releasing Drew's wrist. "You figured right. Okay, let's do this."

They made their way up onto the porch, and Drew knocked on the door, then they stood back and waited. Finally, he could hear footsteps approaching and the door opened to reveal a plump, dark-skinned man who was wearing a long forest-green robe. "Can I help you?" he asked.

"Hi, I'm looking for a man named . . ." Drew looked down at his notes to ensure he got this right. "Grand Master Bartholomew Kensington. I need to speak to him."

"I'm sorry, but there's no one of that name here." He began to close the door, but Drew jumped forward and stopped it from closing.

"Please! It's important! I *need* to speak to him, or if he's not here, another wizard. Just someone who can help me."

"Wizards?" the man said, his eyes turning shifty. "Who told you anything about there being wizards here?"

Drew flushed, not wanting to admit to googling them. He waved at the very wizardish robes the man was wearing. "It kinda looks like there are wizards here. Please, is there anyone who can help me?"

"Sorry, kid. If you're after a love potion, try Etsy."

Before he could try to shut the door again, Zach stepped forward. His eyes darkened and red flame seemed to swirl within them. When he spoke, his voice had an otherworldly quality to it. "He's not after a love potion," he growled.

The robed man's eyes widened and he stepped back, his arms coming up in defense even though Zach hadn't threatened him. Golden wisps of light sprung from his hands, and the hair on Drew's arms rose up from the power he could feel emanating from him, as if a storm were approaching. "Keep back, demon!"

"Simon?" a voice called from inside. "What's going on?" A imposingly tall bald man with an immaculate goatee and bright green eyes came down the hallway. He was also wearing dark green robes but the hood of his had a yellow lining.

"We're under attack, Grand Master!" Simon cried, fearful but determined eyes on Zach.

"Oh, for fuck's sake," Zach growled, allowing his eyes to return back to their usual whiskey colouring. "I am *not* attacking you, you moron! We've come to ask for assistance."

"And what assistance could one of the minions of Hell require from me?" Kensington asked in a deep baritone as smooth as honey.

"I'm no minion," Zach said sharply, but didn't elaborate.

Kensington studied him for a moment and then turned towards Drew, and his eyes widened in surprise. Then he frowned thoughtfully and opened the door wider. "I think you should both come in. Welcome to our humble abode, otherwise known as the Island Chapter of the Nightingale Collective"

The golden wisps still swirling atop Simon's palm dimmed and then flickered out of existence as he stood back, clearly not happy about these developments but trusting Kensington's decision.

They followed the Grand Master inside to a large entrance hall where an imposing staircase led to an upper level. Drew did a double take at the staircase since the house *definitely* hadn't had a second storey on the outside. Kensington noticed his shock but said nothing, just gestured him forward. Drew heard Zach mutter, "A police telephone box is way cooler," as they both followed the wizard.

They skirted the staircase and went down a long hallway instead, ending up in a plush, old-fashioned sitting room. "Tea?" Kensington offered as he took a seat in a large armchair.

Zach sat on the sofa and Drew hurried to sit next to him, feeling safer next to the demon, which he realised was a ridiculous thought. He nodded at Kensington's offer and then watched in amazement as the teapot that was sitting on a sideboard lifted of its own accord and poured three cups of tea. "Just like in *Beauty and the Beast*," Drew whispered.

Zach sniggered and even Kensington's lips twitched, but he didn't look away as the final cup was filled to the brim.

It was only then Drew realised Simon had not joined them, but he couldn't recall precisely when he'd disappeared. "So, you really are a wizard?" he asked in awe as the cups soared across the room to each of them.

"There are many names for my profession, but sorcerer is the most accurate one," Kensington corrected him. "Due to several factors, including my personal power, longevity, and battle experience, I have gained the rank of Grand Master. That means I am not only the leader of our chapter here on the Island, but the entirety of the North West American district. I also have a seat on the World Council."

"So why do you live in Ladysmith of all places?" Drew asked, confused. It seemed like a nice place, but not really somewhere prestigious enough for a man of Kensington's qualifications.

"The cinnamon buns at the bakery are to die for," Kensington said in a prim tone, making it clear he was not going to discuss his actual reasons with them. He sipped his tea. "And who would you be, young man?" he enquired.

"Oh, sorry. I'm Drew . . . Drew Phillips, and this is Zach."

"Zach? I see." Kensington raised an eyebrow at this and Drew wondered if all handsome men with power and an extra dose of self-confidence did the sexy eyebrow thing. "An unusual name for a demon."

"I'm an unusual demon."

"So I see." Kensington's eyes dropped down until they fell on Zach's chest.

Zach stared at him in a silent challenge, but Kensington let it drop.

"So, Mr Phillips, how is it that you came to associate with one such as Zach here?"

"Well, it was an accident, really. I was making soup and he suddenly just appeared."

Kensington set aside his teacup, the porcelain clinking against the saucer. "Soup?" he asked in disbelief.

Drew nodded. "Chicken noodle, if that makes any difference."

Beside him, Zach snorted. "Drew, perhaps you should tell him which recipe you were following, or better yet, show him the book. It'll make more sense then."

"Oh, yes. I can do that!" He rummaged in his backpack and pulled out Grammy's recipe book, glad he'd thought to bring it along. He handed it over and watched as the sorcerer examined it.

"Interesting," Kensington mused. "There is much power in this spell book."

"So Zach said. I never knew Grammy was a witch," Drew admitted.

"The kid has power," Zach told Kensington, crossing his arms over his chest. "Lots of it. It's been a long time since anyone was strong enough to summon me and he did it by accident." He threw Drew a fond look. "But he's untrained, and had no clue about the existence of magic until now."

Kensington stood and crossed the room to them. "May I?" he asked Zach, and something seemed to pass between them. Eventually, Zach nodded, and Kensington reached out, one hand hovering over the demon's head, the other against his chest, not quite touching. He muttered a few words which sounded like complete gobbledygook to Drew and there was a flash of golden light. He repeated the words again, then again, but both times nothing happened apart from the flash of light. Finally, he stepped back, looking perplexed. "It would appear that even the Grand Master would not be powerful enough to summon you." His eyes turned to Drew. "May I?" he asked once more.

"Um, what are you going to do?" Drew asked warily.

"I simply wish to get a reading of your power."

"I really don't think I have any power. I'm just an ordinary person," he argued.

A warm hand landed on his thigh, squeezing briefly. "You're anything but ordinary, Drew," Zach told him.

"Do you think it's safe?" he asked him, knowing he was probably being rude but doing it anyway.

"I won't let Grand Master Kensington or anyone else harm you, Drew. You have my word," Zach promised.

If Kensington found it odd that Drew had sought out a demon's assurances, he didn't show it. Instead, at Drew's nod to him, he simply stepped forward and did much the same to Drew as he'd done to Zach. Other than a tingling feeling all over, Drew felt nothing at all, but Kensington was pale and shaking when his hands dropped, and he almost staggered as he turned back to his chair. He sank into it, breathing hard.

"What did you find?" Zach demanded.

"Raw, untapped power," Kensington uttered.

"Strong?" Zach asked.

Kensington nodded once. "Oh, yes." He swallowed, and in the sudden silence, Drew heard his throat bob.

"How strong?" Zach demanded.

Kensington glanced over at Drew, and he was surprised to see fear in those green eyes. "Stronger than I've ever seen in all my years," he whispered. "Strong enough to destroy the very world."

The silence that fell over the room was charged, and Drew looked between the two men in disbelief. "No fucking way!"

Zach glanced over at Drew as they made their way down the front steps and back onto the sidewalk. He'd hardly said a word for the last half an hour and was still quiet and pensive, but Zach couldn't figure out if it was in a good or a bad way. Was Drew just processing the fact he had powerful magic in his lineage that had manifested intensely within him? Or was he beginning to question his sanity? Was he on the verge of bolting? Was he having regrets that this had ever happened? Zach found it immensely frustrating that he couldn't get a read on the situation, especially as that little flicker of hope had bloomed into a much larger flame.

Drew was powerful . . . *extremely* powerful. This meant there was a very good chance he'd be able to break the bonds of the gem, the bonds that kept Zach a prisoner to Oberon. Kensington didn't know the spell needed to return Zach, however, he was confident that with some training, Drew would master his powers enough to be able to send him back without needing the actual spell itself. Few magic users were strong enough to manage that, but Kensington had no doubts Drew would be one of them.

Zach just had to convince Drew to free him instead of returning him.

Which would mean Zach would likely have to come clean about what he actually was. It was a painful story, one he wasn't keen to have to retell, but if his future rested on the telling, then tell it he would. Luckily, it would appear he had time on his side. Drew wouldn't master his powers overnight, and so Zach had a little time before he'd have to bare his soul—quite literally.

"You okay, kid?" he asked, bumping their shoulders together as they came to a halt in the bright sunshine.

"Hmmm?" Drew asked, looking up. His eyes cleared a little and he offered a small smile. "Oh, sorry. Yeah, I'm good. Just a lot to take in, ya know?"

"I bet." Zach gestured down the street. "It's a pretty nice day. How 'bout we take a walk before going back? I do believe we passed a sign on the way here that said this street once won Canada's Greatest Street. I'm not sure what constitutes a 'great street' but if it has anything to do with the bakery and cinnamon buns Kensington spoke of, I definitely think we need to check it out."

That earned him the shy smile he'd been going for. Drew really was beautiful. The bright sun made his pale blue eyes appear almost translucent, and his unruly hair fell over his face, softening the sharp angles caused by malnutrition. Even though Drew was probably the most powerful person he'd ever met, Zach found himself wanting to protect him at all costs. He had the strongest urge to pull him into the protective circle of his arms and not let him go. Instead, he placed a hand on the small of Drew's back and turned him until they faced downhill, and they began to walk.

The headquarters of the Nightingale Collective was a couple of hundred metres up the road from the business district, and it didn't take long until they'd left the houses behind and were walking past various storefronts. Colourful banners hung from light poles, and hanging baskets overflowing with flowers added splashes of colour. It was busy, with almost every parking space taken, and the sidewalks were crowded with people. The largest crowd was a long queue of customers waiting to get into the bakery.

"Holy crap," Drew murmured as they joined the end of the line. "How good are these buns?"

A woman in front of them heard him and turned with a grin. "You've not had one before?" she asked.

Drew shook his head.

"Oh, honey, you are in for a treat!" she declared. "Do you like cinnamon and cream-cheese frosting?"

Zach wasn't imagining the wistful look in Drew's eyes. "My mom used to make cinnamon buns for me when I was really little. I haven't had one since she died but she always used cream-cheese frosting on them."

The woman's eyes softened and she reached out and squeezed his arm in comfort. "I think these buns will serve your mom's memory well. I hope you enjoy them."

Drew gave her a tight smile and then fell silent once she turned back to her friend. Zach stood a little closer, offering silent support, and they quietly watched the other customers as they inched forward. Once they got through the front door, a heavenly smell hit their noses and they both moaned a little. "I think," Zach said, eyes lingering on the end of the display case where a rapidly dwindling supply of cinnamon buns sat. "We need to get one for now, and then get one for later."

Drew just nodded.

They finally reached the counter and a bubbly young lady asked for their order. They decided on a plain almond and cream-cheese bun each for now, and orange and poppy seed buns to take back home for after dinner. Zach happily handed over his card and soon they had a small white box each in hand with their prizes inside.

Heading back outside into the sunshine, they wandered randomly from store to store, window shopping as they ate. Suddenly, Drew frowned and moved towards a brown-brick building just up from the bakery. Zach followed, but couldn't see anything exciting in the windows at all. In fact, it looked to be empty. "What is it?" he asked.

Drew pointed up. "It's lined with swastikas!" he said, outraged.

"And?" Zach asked.

Glaring, Drew hissed, "I know you're a demon and all, but surely even *you* can see the issue here?"

Zach frowned, thinking hard, and then it clicked. "Oh! Because of the whole Nazi thing."

Were those lasers shooting out of Drew's eyes? "Yes, because of the whole *Nazi thing*," Drew said, the finger quotes not at all necessary to convey his sarcasm. Given he was still holding a box in one hand and the fingers of his other were covered in frosting, they were rather distracting. Would Drew punch him if Zach leaned forward and sucked those fingers into his mouth?

Probably.

"This building looks pretty old. I'm pretty sure it predates the Nazis." Zach scanned the walls and saw a small plaque. He skimmed it and grunted in triumph. "Yep, it was built in 1913. I missed the whole multiple World Wars business, but many of my colleagues were kept very busy with them. You do know the Nazi party appropriated the symbol and turned it evil, but it was actually a holy symbol for many religions for well over ten thousand years."

"Really?"

Zach nodded. "Yeah. It was a symbol of hope."

"Oh, that's sad," Drew said, his righteous anger deflating from him. "True to form, though, I suppose. They ruined so much for so many people." He gave Zach a cautious look. "Being a demon, you're probably the leader of their fan club or something, aren't you?"

He scoffed. "No fucking way. There are some things even too evil for me. I'm glad those fuckers are in the deepest depths of Hell, getting what they deserve."

Drew relaxed at that and his shy smile returned. "I keep forgetting you haven't actually been on Earth for so long. Honestly, how do you know so much about what it's like here?"

They began walking again, heading downhill towards the lower end of the street. "At first I learned from stories, told from those who had been summoned. Some of them brought back books with them, and I'd read everything I could. Then someone brought back a wireless radio and I would tune in each day to listen. Then television. But the internet opened it right up. I could live vicariously through that, learning about anything and everything. Watching videos and shows made me almost feel like I'd actually experienced it for myself."

Drew hummed. "So, you really can't leave Hell unless you're summoned?"

"No, and that's a good thing."

"It is?"

"If we could leave anytime we wanted, this world would have been destroyed long ago." He paused, wondering how to phrase what he wanted to say. "Drew . . . I'm not *like* other demons. You're extremely lucky you accidentally summoned me and not one of the others. I'm an anomaly." He shuddered at the thought of what could have happened to this sweet kid if it had been literally anyone else but him.

Drew looked at him for a long moment, assessing, and then he smiled, lighting up his entire face. "Well then, I'm glad I was lucky enough to get you."

They shared a smile under the bright summer sun, and for the first time in eons, Zach felt . . . happy. He had done some terrible, terrible things in his very long life—things that would horrify Drew—but right now, in this very moment, Zach didn't feel like his soul was weighed down by those actions. He didn't feel the creeping, persistent *guilt* that had prevailed over him, day in, day out, since Oberon had chained him with the power of the gem. Drew made him feel free, and perhaps if he was very, very lucky, he might one day soon actually *be* free.

"Is that a Timmy's?" Drew asked, peering down the road.

Zach glanced further down the street and nodded. "It does appear to be one."

"Could we maybe get a drink?" Drew asked, tentatively. "If that's okay?"

"I thought you weren't a fan of Canada's iconic coffee chain?" he teased.

Drew blushed and shrugged. "It's not *all* bad. It's a nice day, so I thought maybe we could get a cold brew?"

Zach grinned and linked his arm with Drew's. "That sounds delightful. Lead the way."

They had used a rideshare service to get to Ladysmith, since the buses were infrequent and time-consuming, and they called for another to take them back to Nanaimo. Zach glanced at his watch as they slid into the back seat and saw it was past midday. They'd gotten their coffees and wandered back up First Avenue, stopping by the thrift store and reading the plaques on the historic buildings for another hour. Zach was about to suggest they grab some lunch when they got back into town, when Drew's phone pinged with a message. He pulled it out and frowned a little as he read it and then cut his eyes to Zach.

"What is it?" Zach asked.

"Oh, Gwen and Dom are going out tonight for drinks with some of the others and they wanted me to come along."

"Do you not want to go?"

"No, it's not that, a drink would be kinda nice after the past week. It's just . . ." He trailed off and couldn't meet Zach's eyes.

"It's just that I'd have to come along and since there's no way you could explain bringing a cat along, I'd have to come in this form," Zach finished for him.

Drew chewed on his lower lip and nodded. "Yeah."

Not entirely sure of the reasons behind Drew's reluctance—and ignoring the pang of hurt as he worried that Drew was ashamed of him—Zach decided to make an offer instead. "It'll be a bit difficult, but I can try and stay ten feet away the whole night? I could follow you in and find a seat close by but far enough away that you'd have privacy with your friends. It'll be tricky to make sure we don't get separated, since it would be hard to explain us getting yanked back together by the tether, but if the bar they've picked is small enough that we can stick close to one another but busy enough I'm not noticed by your friends, we could make it work."

Drew's brow furrowed. "Why would we do that?"

Zach gestured with his hand, hoping to encompass everything he was trying—and failing—to articulate. "Well, so you can have a night out."

"Why can't you be part of that night out? Do you not want to come along? I thought you might need a drink as well after today."

The flutter in Zach's stomach was ridiculous. He was aware of the attraction Drew felt for him of course, but the mere thought that Drew might *want* to spend time with him was altogether different. "Yes, I'd like to go," Zach told him. "I just thought you might not want me to be there."

The look Drew directed at him spoke volumes about what he thought of Zach's intelligence. "Of course I *want* you to be there."

"Then why the conflicted face?"

Drew sighed and looked away. "You know why."

"I really don't."

There was a long moment of silence as Drew battled with his thoughts, and then he said in a rush, "Because people will wonder who you are and what you're doing there with me. They'll ask if we're dating."

"So?" Zach placed his hand on Drew's knee and squeezed gently. "Why would that be a problem?"

"I've told you before," Drew said. "No one will believe that someone like me managed to land someone as hot as you."

Suppressing the smile at hearing Drew say out loud he thought he was hot, Zach said, "I don't think you're as far out of my league as you think you are, Drew. In fact, I'd say you'd definitely be drafted."

Drew rolled his eyes at the extended sports metaphor but didn't reply.

"If it makes you uncomfortable, we can tell them we're just friends," Zach offered.

"Well, we *are* just friends," Drew said, sounding almost bitter about it.

"So what's the problem?"

Drew's face flushed crimson and after a long pause he admitted in a small voice, "I don't want to have to watch other people trying to pick you up."

"Is that so?" Zach tried not to sound smug about it, knowing it would just further embarrass Drew, but he was extremely pleased about the sentiment. He gave Drew's knee another squeeze. "Don't worry, you're the only one I'll be going home with."

"Yeah, because we physically can't be separated," Drew muttered.

He grinned widely but didn't respond. It seemed like the evening was going to be alive with opportunity. He'd all but lost the desire to keep his hands to himself, and now he had concrete proof Drew wouldn't be opposed to him getting a little handsy. He leaned back in his seat and began to plot.

A Sinful Evening Out

The bar was dimly lit, the music was loud, and there was a crowd of people. Drew surveyed the room, looking for his friends, acutely aware of Zach at his side. The demon was dressed in a sharp suit, and despite it being more formal than the usual dress code for such an establishment, he didn't look out of place at all. Drew's mouth had watered when Zach had emerged from the bathroom, and to cover his arousal he'd made a remark about not wanting to know exactly where Zach kept his wardrobe since he'd not arrived with a suitcase. Zach had laughed and winked and then ushered him out of the apartment, plucking Drew's phone from his hand and bringing up the rideshare app to order them another ride. On the drive over they had discussed what they'd tell Drew's friends about how they knew each other, settling on Zach being a new neighbour so they could explain arriving and leaving together.

Catching a glimpse of Gwen in the far corner of the bar, wearing a sparkly red dress and towering heels, Drew began to head in that direction and then faltered when he also caught sight of Edward. He hadn't known his old high-school bully had been invited along tonight, and if he had, chances were he'd have turned down the invitation. He'd been looking forward to having a few drinks and relaxing, but with Edward here, he'd be constantly on guard for the next verbal attack, the next arrogant and cutting remark.

Zach stopped with him, his eyes following Drew's, and one of his hands came to settle on his lower back. "Problem?" he asked.

Sighing, Drew shook his head. "No, it's fine."

Zach didn't look convinced. "You worried about that douche?" He tilted his head in Edward's direction.

"I just wanted to be able to relax," Drew said. "Don't worry, I've gotten quite good at ignoring him over the years."

"Years?" Zach asked, his eyes narrowing. "You have a history with him?"

"Yeah," Drew said with a nod. "We used to go to high school together. He's gotten better since then. Like, he doesn't get physical anymore, but he just never gives me a break."

A flicker of flame danced over Zach's whiskey-coloured eyes like it had that morning when he was challenged by Simon. "He hurt you?" he growled. "Put his hands on you?"

Biting his lip, Drew nodded. "Mostly just pushing and shoving, but he gave me a black eye once when he shoved me into a pole." He saw Zach's nostrils flare and hurried to add, "But as I said, that kind of crap has stopped now."

Zach took a deep breath to compose himself, and the flames died away. In a much calmer voice, he suggested, "How 'bout we hit the bar first? Get a drink before we join them?"

Drew quickly agreed. Dealing with Edward would be easier with a bit of booze in his system.

Zach had a knack for getting served quickly, and Drew couldn't quite figure out if he was using his magic to influence the bartender or if people were simply naturally drawn to him. He supposed he didn't care much when they didn't have to stand and wait for ten minutes in the queue. He tried to order the cheapest beer they had on tap, conscious of how little he could actually afford to blow on a night out, but Zach wasn't having any of it. He ordered them both two glasses each of expensive bourbon, and they downed one quickly before moving away from the bar with their second drink.

"Okay, let's do this," Drew said, straightening his back and moving with false confidence towards the corner in which his friends—and Edward—were sitting on stools around a high cocktail table.

He was greeted with smiles and hollers from most of the group, and he grinned back at them, but Edward noticed Zach immediately and a predatory look stole over his face. His lips twisted into a sneer and he slid off his stool, stepping towards them. "Well, well, well, look what the cat dragged in." His eyes fell on Zach, assessing. "Who's this? I didn't think you could afford to hire *company* for the evening, Phillips."

Drew swallowed hard and tried to keep his face blank. "He's not a hooker, Edward. This is Zach . . . a friend of mine."

Edward let out a short bark of laughter. "Yeah, sure, Phillips. You're not the sort to have friends like this."

Beside him, Drew was sure he heard Zach growl again, but when he glanced over at him, he didn't look upset. Then one of Zach's arms snaked around Drew's waist and pulled him close. "Okay, you got us. We're not exactly *friends*," Zach said and leaned over to press a kiss to Drew's cheek. "We're quite a bit more than that."

Drew felt himself blushing, but at least the dim lighting would hide it. What was Zach doing? They'd agreed on a cover story and it didn't include fake dating! He reached down to pinch Zach's arm, but all Zach did was pull him even closer against him.

"You're seeing each other?" Dom asked, eyeing Zach. He then winked at Drew. "Damn, Drew, he's hot. Nice!"

"*He's* right here!" Drew protested, causing Dom to laugh at his indignation.

"And I'm well aware of how hot I am," Zach said, waggling his eyebrows in a ridiculous fashion.

"And we're well aware of just how paid for you are," Edward sneered.

Zach shot him a withering look. "You sound like a jealous, petty man-child. It's quite unbecoming."

"Yeah, shut up, Edward," Gwen snapped, and she patted the only remaining stool next to her. "Come and have a seat. I'm sure we can hustle up another one from somewhere."

Zach guided Drew over to the stool and gestured for him to take it. Once Drew had climbed onto it, Zach stood behind him, chest pressed tight to Drew's back, and arms circling his waist. "We're good like this," Zach told Gwen. "No need to find another stool."

"So," she said, sipping her drink. "You gonna introduce us, Drew?"

"Oh, sorry. Everyone, this is Zach. Zach, this is everyone." He took a gulp of his bourbon, unsure of how to proceed.

Gwen just laughed, her blonde hair cascading down over one shoulder. "Helpful, Drew." She waved at Zach. "I'm Gwen. It's nice to meet you."

"Likewise," Zach said, tilting his head. One of his hands had drifted down and he was rubbing small circles onto Drew's thigh with his thumb. It was extremely distracting. But the last thing Drew wanted was for Zach to stop.

"So, how long have you two been together?" she asked them.

"Not too long," Zach said, saving Drew from having to explain and risk giving away the lie. "I moved into the same building a few months back and Drew helped me with some of my furniture. We clicked instantly, and after being oblivious to my advances, I finally just told him I was interested."

Gwen laughed. "That's our Drew. He's rather oblivious to stuff like that." Drew wondered if Zach had been wrong about Gwen also being interested in him, as she didn't seem at all bitter he was seeing someone else.

"Yeah, he is," Zach said, with more fondness than Drew could ever remember anyone directing at him. Soft warm lips pressed against his temple and he felt Zach's nose in his hair. "But you finally got the message, didn't you, sweetness?" He pressed up even closer against him, and Drew was shocked to feel hardness pressing against his ass. *Zach had an erection, and he was making it perfectly clear.*

It was like time came grinding to a halt as Drew processed this. Zach was attracted to him too. Holy shit, it wasn't unreciprocated at all. His breath came out slightly faster, but he managed a smile in Gwen's direction and his hand blindly sought out Zach's. He linked their fingers together and squeezed. "Yeah. It took me a while, but I finally got it."

Zach's lips again pressed against his temple, lingering there, and he could feel when they turned into a smile. "Good," he whispered.

Across the table, Edward rolled his eyes as he took a sip of his beer. Drew felt something a little like a shiver go up his spine and the pressure in the room changed ever so slightly. Suddenly, Edward's beer was spilling down his front, soaking into his expensive, pristine white shirt. He gasped and clunked the half-empty glass down onto the table before grabbing a handful of napkins to mop himself up. Drew heard Zach snicker in his ear. Wondering if it would work when Zach *wasn't* in his cat form, and figuring if it didn't, no one would be the wiser, he thought . . . *Did you do that?*

Of course, Zach's voice replied, loud and clear, but most importantly, silently. *The little shit deserves even worse, but I figured you wouldn't want me to cause too much of a scene.*

Drew grinned. *I wouldn't mind a* little *scene,* he admitted, feeling gleeful. *But yeah, he was being a dick. Thanks for having my back.*

Anytime. Zach pressed another kiss to his hair, and Drew shivered. He wondered whether, by the end of the night, he'd know what those lips felt like on his own? From the way Zach's bulk was still pressed tightly against him, he figured it was a pretty safe bet. Drew almost vibrated with anticipation.

Conversation moved on to other things, and after a while, half the group broke off to get more drinks and Drew downed the rest of his so he and Zach could join them. Zach stayed close by his side, slipping an arm around his waist and inserting his hand into the front pocket of Drew's jeans. It wasn't the only possessive gesture he'd demonstrated throughout the night, and it was far from the last. As they lined up to get their drinks, a girl across the bar began making eyes at Drew. Zach glared at her and immediately slipped further into Drew's space, and then he outright snarled when a guy waiting at the bar next to them tried to give Drew his number. The look of surprise but also fear on the guy's face would have been comical if Drew wasn't so turned on.

An hour later, a tall, gorgeous blonde came over and asked Drew to dance. Zach simply tugged Drew off of the stool he was perched on and led him out onto the dance floor, drawing Drew to him in stark contrast to the fast beat of the music. Reaching up to place his hands on Zach's shoulders, Drew gazed up into amber eyes, seeing his own hunger and arousal mirrored back at him. He swallowed hard and then ducked his head, suddenly shy.

Oh, sweetness, the things I want to do to you, Zach whispered in his mind.

Drew whimpered, the sound lost to the din of the bar, and he pressed his face against Zach's shirt. He inhaled, smelling the spicy cologne the demon wore, bourbon, and a deep, earthy scent that was Zach's natural musk. It was a heady combination, and Drew wished he could bottle it.

Zach's arms tightened around Drew and he moved his hips sinuously, grinding his pelvis against Drew's. His erection was obvious and Drew felt his own cock twitch, having been mostly hard himself the entire evening. With a little encouragement from Zach, Drew began to move his own hips in kind, and they thrust against each other, the bar and the patrons and Drew's friends fading into the background, each other their only focus.

Their movements would have been labelled obscene if they were anywhere else, but here no one judged them, simply watched with envy as they practically devoured one another.

Drew finally looked up, and he was immediately caught by Zach's gaze. The demon's lips twitched a little as he dropped his hands to cup Drew's ass, pulling their hips even closer together and thrusting harshly, and Drew gasped in shock as an orgasm was ripped from him suddenly. His knees went weak and wobbly, and it was only Zach's grip holding him upright that kept him on his feet. His eyes fluttered as he rode out the waves of pleasure rolling over him and his hands tightened into fists in Zach's shirt.

Before he could even recover, Zach was suddenly dragging him from the dance floor, through the crowd, and towards the men's room. The door banged against the tiles as he flung it open, and he ignored the two strangers at the urinals as he strode across the floor with Drew in his grasp and into one of the cubicles on the far side.

"Fuck, sweetness, you have no idea," Zach whispered, and his deft fingers undid the button on Drew's jeans so he could tug them down over his hips. "Want to taste you so bad." And he sank to the filthy floor of the restroom and dragged his tongue up over the mess on Drew's stomach.

An unintelligible sound made its way from Drew's throat as he stared down in wonder at Zach on his knees. His tongue was hot and wet and slightly rough as it moved over the sensitive skin, and the sight of Zach swallowing greedily made Drew's cock twitch and valiantly try to rise again. It was the work of but a minute for the demon to lick him clean, and then he was getting to his feet, helping Drew pull up his jeans and tuck himself away.

"What about you?" Drew mumbled as Zach did up the zipper of his jeans.

Zach smiled, almost gently, and he cupped a hand around Drew's neck and drew him close until their lips brushed, once, twice, almost like butterfly kisses. "I got what I needed tonight," he said before leaning forward and kissing Drew again, deeper this time.

Drew got lost in the kisses and soon the guilt for not reciprocating faded. Zach seemed to genuinely not mind, and it soon seemed unimportant. The only thing that mattered was the next kiss, the next sweep of tongue and nip of teeth. It was better than Drew had imagined, and although he knew it was a little hypocritical, he prayed to God he hadn't gotten drunk and passed out and was only dreaming of this encounter with his demon.

After what seemed to be an eternity but simultaneously not long at all, Zach pulled back, breaking the kiss. "Your friends will wonder where we are," he murmured.

"Let them wonder," Drew said and stole another kiss.

Zach chuckled, low and dirty, but he turned and unlocked the cubicle door and pulled Drew out. Looking up, Drew caught sight of himself in the mirror looking flushed and sated, and a second later he recognised the fair hair of the man at the urinal and flinched as Edward turned to look at them. Edward looked surprised but then he smirked, a mean tilt to his mouth as he crossed to the basin. "Well, well, well, if it isn't little Drew Phillips, deflowered at last."

Before Drew could retort, Zach pulled Drew up against his chest, an arm winding possessively around his waist. "You seem bitter that it isn't *you* who's in my place right now," Zach commented, a dangerous edge to his voice. "Best get over that, boy. I don't share." Then he was moving, guiding Drew out of the washroom and into the dark, dimly lit bar.

Confession

S omething was moving across Zach's body, and he woke, but he didn't move or open his eyes as he assessed the threat. It didn't take long to determine what it was, especially as a hot, wet tongue licked up across his stomach, finding its way to one of his nipples where it twirled inexpertly around it. "Drew?" he murmured, keeping his eyes closed.

"Hmmm?" Drew responded, not ceasing his exploration.

"Whatcha doing, sweetness?"

"Just making sure we're even," he replied.

At that, Zach opened his eyes and raised his head so he could peer down at him. Drew was avoiding his gaze, concentrating on the bare skin of Zach's chest and stomach, and he was blushing, his inexperience written plainly on his face. He reached down to palm the bulge at the front of the tight black boxer briefs Zach wore, but it wasn't firm enough to do much more than lightly tease. Something twisted sharply in Zach's stomach and he reached down and tugged Drew upwards until he was lying comfortably in Zach's embrace. "What did I tell you, Drew? Hmmm?" he asked softly.

Drew's reply was a confused quirk of his brows.

"I told you that you don't owe me anything . . . that I'd never extort anything from you."

"But this is different, isn't it?" Drew mumbled.

"No, it's not. Hey, look at me, sweetness." He gently took hold of Drew's chin and tilted his head until their eyes met. "What happened last night was just as good for me as it was for you." He held a finger to Drew's lips as he began to protest. "Sex isn't about keeping score of orgasms, okay? It's as much about finding enjoyment in the pleasure of your partner as it is about the physical pleasure you receive yourself. I enjoyed last night very much, there's no doubt about that. Do I want to do more? Of course, I do, but I want us to take our time . . . to savour it. I want to be able to savour *you*. Do you understand what I'm saying?"

Drew nodded slowly, but his pale blue eyes were still puzzled. "I do, but . . ."

"But what?"

"Well, it's just that, to be completely honest . . ." He trailed off once more.

"You can talk to me, Drew. I want to do right by you."

"That's just it!" he exclaimed. "You're a *demon*, Zach! Demons aren't supposed to want to *do right* by people! It's weird and confusing!"

This was it. Time to come clean, to tell the truth. *Fuck.* He'd been running from the truth for so long now, it was going to be painful to relive it once more. "That's not *technically* true," he admitted.

Drew cocked his head to one side as he regarded Zach. "What's not technically true?"

Zach took a deep breath and ripped off the metaphorical bandaid. "The part about me being a demon. Technically, I'm not."

Drew's brow furrowed even further. "Oookay," he said, drawing it out. "So what *are* you, then?"

"It's a bit of a long story," Zach said.

"I have time." He shifted pointedly, getting more comfortable against Zach's chest. *Settling in.*

Sighing, Zach prepared himself to tell the story of his betrayal and his consequential fall from grace. The feel of Drew in his arms brought him some measure of comfort, however, and as he began to speak, he found it easier to tell his story than he thought it would be. "Once upon a time—a very, *very* long time ago—I was actually an angel." Drew's eyes widened in surprise, but he didn't interrupt. "I'm sure you figured out that if one side existed, then the other side would have to exist as well. It's not quite like the major religions of the world would have you believe, but they got the names right, at least. There are angels and there is a God, though they aren't a man, nor are they a woman. They are just *Them,* a being of immense power that oversees the creation and evolution of life on all of the planets."

Drew sucked in a breath, probably to ask about that final statement, but then he let it go, and as if it was taking all of his willpower, he held his tongue.

"I didn't ever meet Them myself, very few of us did. There were higher angels—I guess you could compare them to upper management—and they were the ones who did the day-to-day running of Heaven." He smiled wryly. "It was all very corporate when I think about it. Anyway, one of those upper-management angels, Oberon, was like an uncle to me. He took me under his wing, quite literally, and taught me all he knew. I think he was training me to become like him, but I didn't think much of it, being too caught up in the work I was doing. I got so involved in my projects that I became oblivious to all that was happening around me, and so I didn't see what Oberon was doing until it was too late. He had a plan to seize power from Them, to become the supreme ruler of the universe, but he was discovered and he was judged. During his trial, he threw me under the metaphorical bus, telling the court I was also involved . . . that I was in partnership with him."

"They surely didn't believe that, did they?" Drew asked, aghast.

Zach shook his head. "No, they didn't, not really. They announced that I'd be kept under watch and supervised until such time as they could determine with accuracy that I was trustworthy, but Oberon would suffer another fate. He was to be stripped of his wings and then he was to Fall."

"Fall?"

Zach swallowed loudly. "The Fall was the worst punishment that could be meted out to an angel. It meant banishment from Heaven, to be exiled to Hell, to the Underworld, for all eternity. To no longer be an angel but become a demon instead. I was made to watch as Oberon's wings were hacked off—a warning I suppose, for what would be in store for me if my heart was as black as his. Afterward, as he lay there shaking and bleeding, he begged to be able to speak with me one last time. He confessed I was innocent, that I'd had nothing to do with his schemes, and told them he wished to beg for my forgiveness. Compassion is one of an angel's virtues, and so they granted his request. He gestured for me to come closer and I did, eager to hear the apology for his betrayal." Zach fell silent for a moment, and his eyes closed as he relived the next moments once more in the privacy of his own mind. When he opened them again, Drew was watching him with kind eyes and linking their fingers together, feeding Zach the strength to continue. "Oberon had no intention of apologising. He grabbed me instead, locking my wings by my side with his arms so I was unable to fly, and then he jumped, taking me with him."

Drew gasped but didn't press for more, granting Zach the time he needed.

"What happened when we reached the bottom does not bear repeating. Suffice to say, an angel who finds himself in Hell is not in for a pleasant time."

"The others," Drew said, frowning. "They didn't come to rescue you? They knew you were innocent."

Zach shrugged. "If they tried, they did not succeed. I never saw any of them ever again. Oberon embedded this gem in my chest and it binds me to him and prevents me from escaping the confines of Hell. Only the most powerful magic users have ever been able to summon me, and none of them have ever been able to break its hold on me." Zach took a deep breath and then met Drew's eyes. "Until now, Drew. I truly believe *you* have that power. I think you'll be able to free me from Oberon's grasp."

"Me?" Drew squeaked. "I don't know anything about magic!"

"I know, but Kensington said you have immense power within you. I believe with some training from Kensington, who will be able to help you master that power, you'll be able to break my bonds. I suppose the question remains . . . Do you want to?"

Drew looked at him in astonishment and shook his head. "Are you fucking insane?" he demanded. "Why the hell *wouldn't* I want to help you, Zach? Of course I freaking will!"

Zach relaxed at the words. Being almost certain was very different from knowing for sure and he hadn't realised how tense that had been making him. "Thank you," he whispered and then leaned forward to capture Drew's mouth in a soft kiss.

"You know this explains an awful lot, don't you?" Drew said a little smugly, as he pulled back.

"What do you mean?" Zach asked.

"Well, to be brutally honest, you're a really shitty demon," Drew said, grinning. "Like, you are *way* too nice. Nowhere near evil enough."

Zach laughed and conceded the point. "I must admit, there are things I've done since the Fall that were not at all angelic, but one does what one needs to survive, I suppose. I had no way to escape and certain things were expected of me if I wanted to live, and so I did them. I never took pleasure in them, though, not the truly awful things anyway. Morals do get a little hazy after such a long time and I doubt I will ever be welcomed back up top, but my hope is to be able to stay here, in this place." The *with you* he left unsaid, unsure if Drew would even be interested in anything long term with him. As far as Drew had been aware, this was a limited-time-only deal, and maybe he preferred it that way. He would have to cross that bridge when he got to it.

"Can I ask a question?" Drew asked.

"Of course."

"What happened to your wings?"

"Oh, those."

Drew suddenly looked ill. "Oh, fuck, did they cut them off? When they did those horrible things to you?"

Zach shook his head. "No. Yes, they used them to hurt me, but they didn't cut them off. Not to say they didn't try, but for some reason, the only blade that has ever been able to sever wings from an angel is the one used by the most senior of the higher angels. No, they kind of just . . . faded. It took a long time as they became less and less substantial, until one day they were just gone. I don't think they could survive in that sort of environment."

"Will you ever get them back?" Drew asked.

He shrugged. "No idea."

"Do you miss them?"

He smiled sadly. "Every single day."

"They must have been beautiful," Drew said wistfully.

Zach nodded. "They were. They were magnificent. Each angel's wings are a different colour. They're not all pure white like books and movies would have you believe. Mine were the deepest black you can imagine, but in the light, the feathers were tinged with a deep red."

"They sound amazing. Maybe once I've worked out a way to free you, they'll come back and I'll get to see them for myself?"

Zach smiled, and he leaned in for another kiss. "Maybe."

"Right," Drew said, and he climbed out of bed. "It looks like I've got a lot to learn. Best get to it. Shall we drop by for a visit with the Grand Master and see what he can teach me about tapping into this supposed power of mine?"

Hope welled in Zach's chest, and he had to blink back tears. "I like the way you think, Drew," he whispered, and as he climbed from the bed, for a fleeting moment, he felt the weight of his wings at his back.

Schooled

L earning magic was *hard*. For something he had managed completely by accident, Drew thought it wouldn't take much to tap into it again, but in a controlled manner. He was so very, very wrong.

Sunday had turned out to be bright and warm when they left the apartment, and for a very brief moment, Drew had been tempted to ditch his plans to go and beg Kensington for help and to drag Zach out for a day of fun in the sun instead. The idea of heading up to Parksville to see Todd was tempting. Not only would it be good to see his friend, but the sand-sculpting competition was on and they could spend time down at the beach checking it out. It always left him amazed at the art people could create from simple sand. Todd might even drive them up to Coombs so they could head to the markets there and get an ice cream. Drew could just picture Zach's baffled expression when he saw the goats that lived on the grass-covered roof of the old market building. He would find it so perplexing and Drew would have fun making up absurd stories as to the origins of the goats.

But Zach was depending on him.

So instead of hopping on a bus and heading north, Drew ordered a rideshare and they went south to Ladysmith instead. They knocked on the door of the Nightingale Collective and instead of Simon it was Kensington himself who answered it.

He looked less than impressed to see them there, but he held the door open and welcomed them inside nonetheless. "How can I help you today, Mr Phillips?"

"I'm here to ask for your help," Drew said as they stepped into the large entrance hall.

One of his perfectly manicured eyebrows rose over a bright green eye. Seriously, did he and Zach take classes to learn how to do that? Drew could hardly coordinate both eyebrows at once, let alone one at a time. "What sort of help?" Kensington asked.

"Training. I need training."

Kensington regarded him for a long moment, and Drew was sure that his mettle was being measured and judged. He must have passed the test, as the sorcerer finally nodded. "I can indeed help you there, Mr Phillips. However, you must agree to follow all of my instructions, no matter how tedious you may find them. You must also be dedicated to your studies. I understand you also attend university and therefore will need to split your time between both, but I will not tolerate laziness. If I am to sacrifice my very important time to train you, then I expect your complete dedication to the task. No slacking off, no half-hearted effort, no phoning it in. Do I make myself clear?"

"Crystal clear, Grand Master Kensington."

"Pfft, none of that," he said, flapping a hand in front of him. "Just call me Kensington."

Drew smiled. "Okay. Thanks."

"Let's head down to the workshop," Kensington said and led them down a different hallway than he had the day prior. "There's more room for us to work in there."

"We're starting today?" Drew asked, surprised.

"There's no time like the present. Come on, chop chop."

Drew exchanged a bemused glance with Zach, but they obediently followed him down multiple hallways, proving once again that the building was much larger than it appeared from the outside. They eventually stopped in front of a pair of wide double doors, and Kensington pushed them open, revealing a large, airy room beyond. The vaulted ceiling was high, curving around to meet a windowed dome in the centre which allowed bright sunlight to stream inside and send dust motes dancing. Numerous workbenches were scattered around the room, some covered in leather-bound books, some with smoking beakers and jars full of odd-coloured liquids, and one was completely cleared of all objects but had several chalk symbols etched on the surface. Chairs and stools dotted the room randomly, and every inch of wall space was filled with overflowing bookcases and cabinets with odd-looking trinkets. On one shelf sat a squat clock that ticked loudly in the silence.

Kensington led them inside and directed Zach to a chair to one side of the room and Drew to the nearby table. "I understand the limitations of how far you can be separated from one another," he said to Zach. "But I do ask you do not distract young Mr Phillips from his studies."

Zach merely looked amused at this, and he graciously tilted his head in agreement. "Of course."

"Very well, then," Kensington said and turned back to Drew. "Let us start with the basics. You need to find your centre."

Drew wished he could pull off the single-eyebrow raise so he could level it at Kensington, but had to settle for an incredulous look instead. "Seriously? Like those hippie yoga moms?"

The sorcerer's eyes narrowed. "You agreed to do exactly as I say and yet you question the very first instruction I give you?"

Drew felt a little bad at that. He scrambled for something to excuse his flippancy. "Well, I mean, it just sounds kind of . . . New Agey?"

Taking a deep breath, Kensington visibly gathered his patience. "Your magic sits inside you like a well of power. In order to access it, you need to be able to locate it. To do that, you need to find your centre. Without mastering this first step, you will never have control over your power and you will continue to wield it without aplomb or finesse, likely endangering not only yourself but others. I apologise if this sounds too 'New Agey' for you," he said flatly. "But it is an essential part of the process."

Duly chastised, Drew bowed his head. "Okay, I get it. I'm sorry." He let out a long breath. "So, how do I find my centre?"

Kensington walked him through some breathing exercises very similar to meditation. Drew needed to connect with his body in a way he had never done before, but it seemed that each time he directed his attention inwards, his mind would distract him with thoughts of how silly this all was and how much he was going to fail. He tried to find the spark, the well of power that Kensington assured him was there, in his very core, but it constantly eluded him.

"It's no use," Drew cried after being unsuccessful after another hour of trying. He'd moved around the room, trying different positions, but none had worked. He slumped down against the bookcase he was sitting in front of and buried his face in his hands. "I'm never going to get this."

"This first step is always the hardest," Kensington assured him. "Once you have tapped into your centre once, it will become easier and easier to find until you can access it with the merest of thoughts."

"May I?" Zach asked, speaking for the first time since the training had begun.

Kensington regarded him for a long moment and then waved his acquiescence. "Be my guest."

Zach stood and crossed the short distance to Drew, crouching down in front of him. "You're overthinking this," he told him softly. "Don't be so hard on yourself."

"How can you say that?" Drew demanded. "You have so much riding on this! If I fail at this, I fail you!"

"Oh, sweetness, no. You could never possibly fail me. The fact you're even willing to try is more than anyone has done for me before."

"What if I can't ever find my centre?" he asked, sounding utterly dejected even to his own ears.

"You're putting too much pressure on yourself. You need to relax." Zach reached over and pressed a warm palm to Drew's chest. "Close your eyes and breathe with me."

Drew did as he asked, following Zach's lead as he breathed in and out evenly. He felt his whole body relax and his heart slowed. The warmth of Zach's hand seemed to blossom and spread throughout his body, relaxing him even further.

That's it, Drew, Zach said in his mind. *You're doing great.*

Drew continued to breathe in sync with Zach and his body began to feel heavy. If his eyes weren't already closed, he was sure they would have fluttered shut by now. He didn't worry about that, just concentrated on the next breath, and the next one after that.

Perfect, sweetness. Now, think about your heart and how it's beating so strongly beneath my palm.

It was easy to do. The weight of Zach's touch above his heart was like a beacon, and his mind immediately zeroed in on the spot. He could picture it clearly in his mind's eye, the way the muscle was beating, pumping blood rich with oxygen all around his body.

Now, let's go a little lower, Zach urged, and he slowly slid his hand down Drew's sternum, until it was resting over his diaphragm. *Breath in for me, nice and deep. Feel how your body responds.*

Drew did as he was told and he could feel even more oxygen pumping through his veins, moving throughout his body. Zach's hand moved steadily up and down in time with Drew's breaths, the warmth still radiating from him.

Now, lower still, Zach said, and he dropped his hand just a fraction more until it rested above Drew's abdomen. *Tell me what you see.*

Drew's mind dropped down and he suddenly gasped as he found a glowing mass of power just under his diaphragm. "Oh, wow," he said breathily.

"That's it," Zach murmured aloud. "Well done, sweetness."

His eyes fluttered open and Drew found himself giving Zach a dopey smile. "I found my centre!"

Zach leaned in and gave him a kiss, just a sweet press of their lips. "You did."

"I see things between you have changed rather dramatically since yesterday," Kensington said, bustling over with a pointed look in their direction.

Drew blushed. "Um, yeah."

"Does this mean you've told him the truth of the matter?" the sorcerer asked Zach.

Zach bristled, but nodded. "I did. Not that it's any business of yours."

"On the contrary," Kensington disagreed, "I believe it is very *much* my business, since I'm guessing that was the reason for the request for immediate training."

"Is that a problem?" Drew asked warily.

Kensington shook his head. "Not at all. It actually makes it easier as we have a goal for you to work towards now."

Drew gave him a smile. "Thank you. And yay! I found my centre!"

"Yes, yes, well done to you both. Now, Zach, shoo." Kensington waved him off to the side of the room. "Mr Phillips, it's time to do it again. Now, clear your mind and find your centre."

They spent the entire day at the Nightingale Collective, not returning to the apartment until late that evening. Drew was exhausted and stumbled into the apartment, tripping over his own feet, but somehow he didn't face plant on the floor. He looked up and found Zach watching him fondly, and he had an inkling that the only reason he wasn't on the ground right now was because of a little magical assistance from his angel. Zach gave him no time to ponder this, however, as he guided Drew into bed— but sleep eluded him. His body craved rest, but his mind churned over the knowledge it had been given that day. He decided that Kensington was a sadistic bastard, as he had pushed Drew brutally, never allowing him a moment of weakness, always demanding—and expecting—his best. He'd informed Drew he was to practise every single day, and starting tomorrow he would finish his classes at university and head directly to the Collective for his magical extracurricular. As tired as Drew was after only one day of training, he knew he had to continue to give it his all. Zach's freedom depended on it. So as strict as Kensington was being, maybe he wasn't such a bastard after all. He wasn't charging Drew for his time and hadn't asked for anything but his dedication to his studies in return. It was almost like he wanted Drew to succeed as much as Zach did.

Eventually, he succumbed to sleep, his body completely spent.

Drew had a full day of classes on Monday so it was well after five p.m. when he arrived at the Collective for his second day of training. Simon greeted them at the door this time and led them through the maze of hallways to the workshop, his forest-green robe flapping around his legs as he walked. Kensington was already there, and he glanced up as they entered. "Good afternoon," he greeted them. He wasn't wearing a robe today but had on plain black trousers and a crisp white button-down that had the sleeves rolled up to the elbows.

"Hi," Drew said, dropping his backpack on the ground by the door and crossing to the bench where the sorcerer was sitting. Several small objects were arranged on the table in front of them, and Drew looked at them curiously. They didn't seem inherently magical, more like basic household objects and small curios which ranged from a porcelain figurine of a dog to a pinecone to a spotted feather, and even a dustpan and brush set.

"Have you been practising finding your centre today?" Kensington asked. He had assigned Drew homework yesterday. At least once an hour, no matter what he was doing, he was to try and find his centre. As Kensington had pointed out, he wouldn't always be in a quiet space when he needed to access his magic, so he needed to get used to doing so in everyday settings.

"I did," Drew confirmed.

"And? How did you fare?"

Drew held up one hand and rocked it back and forth. "Eh, maybe fifty-fifty? Half the time it was relatively easy to find, but other times I kept getting distracted."

"To be expected, so keep it up," Kensington told him. "Today, we'll be working on having you recognise when magic is being used. Just because you cannot use your own power as yet, does not preclude you from being able to recognise when someone else is accessing theirs." He gestured to the items on the table. "Tell me what you observe."

Drew watched as Kensington glanced down at the table and then muttered a word he didn't quite catch. There was a strange pressure in the air that made his ears pop and then the dog figurine rose smoothly into the air.

Drew rubbed at the spot on his neck just below his ear. "It was like the pressure in the room changed." He looked over at Zach, who had taken a seat in a comfortable-looking armchair and was flipping through a book. "I've noticed that happen a few times lately. Was that you doing magic?"

"It was," Zach confirmed, looking up from the book with a smile.

"Huh."

"Sometimes it will be quite subtle, but there will always be that slight change in atmospheric pressure when magic is being used," Kensington continued. "The greater the magic being used, the greater the change in pressure."

"So magic actually affects the atmospheric pressure itself?" Drew asked in surprise.

"It does," Kensington confirmed. "Though we're not entirely sure how."

"It's why some storms are magically charged," Zach added. "I've not been around these past centuries to know of any recent incidents, but I've been there before when a whole village was destroyed by a tornado which was the result of a magical battle."

"Holy crap," Drew muttered. "How much magic is needed for that? Like, am I going to be causing random weather events by doing this sort of stuff?"

Kensington shook his head. "No, the forces Zach is speaking of are only generated by prolonged use of very strong magic by multiple users at once. A single user could not generate a magical storm themselves, even one as powerful as yourself. Even if all of us, plus Simon, were to use our powers all at once there is very little chance of affecting the weather unless we were doing very powerful spells."

"Well, 'today I learned' I guess."

"That *is* the point of this training," the sorcerer said dryly. "Now, I want you to close your eyes and try to find your centre, but alert me each time you feel me using my magic."

Drew nodded and did what he was told, and his lesson continued.

Two days later, Drew was able to reliably locate the spark of magic deep within himself ninety percent of the time. Zach had helped him practise, transforming into his cat form and weaving around his ankles, batting at his shoelaces with his paws, and meowing loudly in his ear to distract him. He could mostly tune out everything else and concentrate, but some distractions were simply too great. Only time and practice would help him there.

Kensington continued to push him, and he'd had him memorise numerous simple spells which would help direct his magic. Drew had been disappointed to learn most of them were simply directions in Latin and didn't have any deeper meaning. "To be completely honest, the spell itself is simply to guide your magic," Kensington had explained. "If you struggle with Latin, you can always just stick to English, but you'll likely give away to every man and his dog what you're doing."

Today, Kensington decided that Drew was ready to move to the next level and actually *use* his power. "To begin with, I want you to try to lift this brush into the air," Kensington instructed, pointing at the dustpan and brush set on the table.

Drew looked around the room. "Do I at least get to wear a fancy wizard's hat?"

Kensington gave him a disapproving glare. "I may be bald, but does this goatee *look* like a long grey beard to you, Mr Phillips?"

Towering over Drew with his bald head and green eyes, he looked very unlike Yen Sid. "Um, no," Drew admitted.

"Then please do not treat this lesson like an excerpt from an animated children's film from 1940. As I have explained previously when covering magical theory, you access your power by concentrating your willpower on your inherent magic. It is only then that you use a spell or incantation to direct and channel the magic to do your bidding."

Drew nodded. "Ah, so more like the will and the word."

Kensington gave him a withering look. "What are you babbling on about now?"

"*The Belgariad*, by David Eddings," Drew told him. At the sorcerer's blank look, he added, "It's every thirteen-year-old's gateway drug into the world of fantasy fiction. Seriously, you've never read them?"

"They're very good," Simon agreed from where he was sitting, chatting with Zach.

"Why would I waste my time on fictional magic when I can wield my own?" Kensington demanded.

"And yet you not only got the *Fantasia* reference, but you knew the exact year of its release," Drew pointed out.

Clearly at the end of his patience, Kensington pointed at the brush. "However you want to describe your magical ability in the privacy of your own brain is your prerogative, Mr Phillips, but for now, using one of the spells I have taught you, *try and lift the brush.*"

Grumbling under his breath about Kensington's complete lack of humour, Drew stared at the small brush. He found his centre and felt the power sparking beneath his diaphragm, and he caressed it with his thoughts, dipping inside the well of power. Although it wasn't necessary at all, he pointed to the brush and whispered, "Surge sursus."

To his amazement, the brush lifted easily into the air and Drew let out a *whoop* of excitement. Even Kensington looked pleased, and he nodded in encouragement. Arms slid around his waist from behind as Zach hugged him, then said against his ear, "Well done. I'll be sure to reward you later."

Kensington rolled his eyes. "I really didn't need to hear that. Now, if you don't mind, stop distracting him. Mr Phillips has a long way to go yet."

Grinning, Drew pressed a quick kiss to Zach's cheek and then turned back to the items on the table. "Which one next?"

"The baby's shoe," Kensington instructed, and Drew concentrated.

The week had been so very busy that despite sleeping in the same bed each night, Drew and Zach had done nothing more than share the odd kiss since his training had begun. It was now the weekend once more and Kensington had given Drew the evening off after a successful day of study and practice. Dead on his feet, Drew shuffled into the apartment and allowed Zach to guide him directly to the bed where he collapsed and fell immediately into a deep slumber. He didn't know how long he'd napped, but when he woke he was alone in the bed and there was a delicious aroma drifting from the small kitchen. He rolled out of bed, rubbing a hand through his sleep-tousled hair, and wandered through to the kitchen. Zach was standing at the stove, stirring a pot with one hand, while the other was turning the pages of a novel. "Smells good," he mumbled and then yawned widely.Zach twisted to flash him a smile before turning back to check the pot. "You've had a long week. I figured a home-cooked meal would do you good."Drew slumped onto one of the chairs, and rubbed the rest of the sleep from his eyes. "Your week has been just as long as mine," he protested."Hardly," Zach retorted. "I spent the days curled up asleep in your bag in my cat form, and then I lazed about, chatting to Simon and watching you and Kensington in the evenings. It's not exactly been what I'd call strenuous."Drew shrugged. "Yes, but you still didn't have to go to any trouble just for me. Besides, I didn't know you could cook."Zach tapped the wooden spoon against the side of the pot and turned down the heat then came over and stood behind Drew. He pressed a kiss to the top of his head and then began to massage his shoulders. "I *wanted* to do something nice for you; I didn't think I *had* to. And yes, I cook . . . not often, but I'm pretty good at it."Drew's head dropped forward as strong fingers dug into muscles he didn't even realise had been tight. "Of course you're good at this. You're good at *everything,*" he said. Zach laughed and then leaned over him and kissed his cheek. "Why don't you go and have a shower," he whispered against Drew's ear. "Then, after dinner, I can show you a few other things I'm good at." Drew let out a little moan. "That sounds awesome." Zach chuckled and stepped away to allow him up. "Go on, then. Dinner will be done in about ten minutes." Drew headed for the bathroom, almost tripping on a discarded pair of jeans but finding his feet in time. He'd become more and more attuned to the change in pressure surrounding him when magic was being performed thanks to his training, and he'd felt it several times over the past week when his clumsiness had sent him tripping over his feet, or spilling his coffee, or knocking something over. Warmth bloomed in his chest as he realised Zach had been watching over him, sending small tendrils of magic his way to prevent little accidents. No one besides his aunt had ever seemed to care so much about him. Even Todd, his best friend all throughout high school, had laughed at him when he'd been a klutz, teasing him for being so accident prone. It suddenly struck him that he'd only exchanged a couple of texts with Todd since Zach arrived and he started to feel guilty. They usually texted each other several times a day on average, just checking in, sharing memes, or simply sending a quip or in-joke to make the other laugh. Had he been such a shitty friend, getting so caught up in the sexy "demon' he'd accidentally summoned, that he'd not had time for his best friend? But wasn't keeping in touch a two-way street? He'd not texted Todd much, but Todd hadn't been texting him either. They weren't that far from each other—Todd lived in Parksville and was studying his Bachelor of Anthropology at the Parksville-Quallicum Centre, which was only a forty-minute bus ride from Nanaimo—but it was only natural they weren't as close as they had been when they saw each other every single day during high school. When Todd came to visit or Drew went to see him, their friendship felt just as strong as ever, so Drew decided he wouldn't feel guilty about not sending a message every day, and he wouldn't get bent out of shape if Todd didn't either.

This was part and parcel of being an adult, and he could accept that. With that out of the way, he put the worry from his mind and got back to what he was doing.Stripping out of his clothes, Drew turned the water on and waited for it to heat up. He caught sight of his reflection in the mirror and raised a hand to his ribs, letting it dance across his chest. The hollows between his ribs weren't as deep, and his stomach wasn't anywhere near as concave as it had been even a week prior. Seven days of eating three meals a day, plus snacks, was putting meat back on his bones, and that was yet another thing he had to be grateful to Zach for. He'd made such a positive impact on Drew's life already that even if he hadn't been told about Zach's past, there was no way Drew would ever have considered him evil. Zach may harbour some regrets about the things he'd been made to do in the past, but he was a good person. Sure, he may technically be an angel masquerading as a demon, but at his core he was inherently *good.*Drew didn't linger in the shower, eager to have some quality time with Zach. The past week had been so hectic that although they were still bound by the ten-foot magical tether, they hadn't actually *spent* much time together. He missed chatting with Zach, exchanging quips, and catching the little hints Zach dropped about what life had been like in Hell for an ex-angel. He was desperate to learn more, but also desperate to explore their physical relationship even more. He'd had just a taste, and he was more than just hungry for Zach—Drew wanted to *devour* him.The table was set, and dinner was dished up—a creamy chicken dish that had Drew's mouth watering. Zach was pouring two glasses of wine and he held one out for Drew to take. Drew accepted the glass but immediately set it on the table so he could pull Zach to him, tilting his head up and seeking out Zach's mouth with his own. The kiss was sweet and lingering, holding such a promise of what was still to come that Drew felt a little dizzy from it. Anticipation built within him but he was happy to savour it, to let it build, to enjoy each excruciating moment. He knew it would simply make what was to come later even better. So he pulled away with a smile, took his seat, and prepared to simply enjoy the meal Zach had prepared.The food was delicious, and Drew was sure he made some rather inappropriate sounds as he ate, but the darkening of Zach's eyes told him he didn't mind one little bit. They spoke of inconsequential things, having entire conversations in movie quotes and pop culture references, and they laughed deeply and often. Once they'd finished eating, Zach waved off Drew's offer to do the dishes, and they settled on the bed with a bowl of popcorn and a movie on the TV. Zach encouraged Drew to sit in the V of his legs and he restarted the massage he'd begun earlier. Drew sighed happily and relaxed even more.Once the massage was finished, Drew stayed where he was and just leaned back to be cradled against Zach's chest. His eyes were on the TV but his fingers danced idly over Zach's legs, just as Zach's hands traced patterns over Drew's stomach. One of his fingers brushed under the hem of Drew's shirt, and the touch of bare skin on bare skin made him shiver. It was easier to be bold when he couldn't see Zach, so Drew sat forward enough so he could pull his shirt off over his head and discard it on the floor next to the bed. He heard Zach huff in amusement, and before he settled back down there was a ruffle of movement and soon Zach's shirt was joining his own on the floor. If the touch of a finger against his bare skin had been shiver inducing, the feeling of his back pressed against Zach's chest was electrifying. Large warm hands ghosted over his stomach and chest, the pads of Zach's thumbs swirling around his nipples, teasing them to small hard peaks. Drew's mouth fell open a little in pleasure—he'd never played with his nipples before and hadn't known they could be so sensitive. Goosebumps covered his skin and he suddenly *needed* to be kissing Zach. He pulled from the embrace and flipped himself over onto his knees, manoeuvring until he was straddling Zach's lap. He linked his hands around the demon's neck—*angel*, get it right, he's actually an *angel*—and leaned forward, capturing Zach's lips with his own. Zach's hands dropped to Drew's hips, his fingers cradling the sharp protrusions of bone, the warmth of them spreading right through Drew. He opened his mouth a little wider, hoping to encourage Zach's tongue inside, and he soon responded, licking his way into Drew's mouth."Fuck, sweetness," Zach almost gasped, pulling away from Drew's lips and peppering his face with light butterfly kisses. "You're so perfect, so fucking perfect." As he spoke, one of his hands moved to the front and began tugging at the strings of the sweats Drew had put on after his shower, and it wasn't long before Zach had freed Drew's cock. He didn't touch it, however, and Drew's head dropped down to Zach's shoulder until he could see him working at the zipper of his own pants. It took a little more manoeuvring before he was able to pull his own cock out, but then he was wrapping his large hand around both of them and Drew lost the ability to think.Zach's cock was steel and silk and wetness and the feeling of it rubbing against Drew's own was indescribable. He'd never felt anything like it before, but he hoped like hell it would be something he'd get to experience many more times in the future. "Zach," Drew moaned, so close already."I know, I know," Zach murmured, kissing his way across Drew's cheek until he was nosing at his ear, taking the lobe between his teeth and tugging on it gently. His hand continued to stroke them, spreading the precum that was leaking between them over both of their lengths.Drew rocked his hips, thrusting into Zach's fist, and he could feel the tension in his muscles as his climax began to build. When he tipped over the edge he cried out, flinging his head backward, unable to watch, only feel."Fuck, Drew, that's it, sweetness, that's it," Zach crooned, and a moment later Drew felt warmth wash over his still-spurting cock as Zach came as well. Then Drew's legs turned to jelly, and he clutched at Zach's shoulders, unable to keep himself upright any longer. Zach chuckled and in one graceful movement he rolled them so Drew was on his back, and then he was off the bed and heading into the bathroom. He returned a short while later with a warm washcloth and wiped Drew's stomach and softening cock gently, removing most of the mess. He then tossed the cloth back in the direction of the bathroom, turned off the DVD they'd been completely ignoring, and climbed into bed, pulling Drew into his arms."That was amazing," Drew uttered, feeling completely blissed out."Yes, it was," Zach agreed. Drew yawned widely, his jaw cracking. "Mmm, tired," he mumbled."You've had a pretty big week," Zach said. "Get some sleep.""'Kay," Drew said. "Oh, just a sec." He opened his eyes and concentrated hard for a long moment and the light flicked off. He grinned. "Nailed it."Zach laughed. "That's my boy. Now sleep.""Sweet dreams, Zach.""I'm sleeping with you in my arms, Drew, *of course* I'm going to have sweet dreams," Zach told him, and Drew fell asleep between one breath and the next, a smile on his face.

On the Sabbath, They Rested

"Will you tell me about your aunt?"

Drew looked up from the snow globe he was examining to find Zach watching him intently. "What do you want to know?" he asked, putting the globe down and moving over to the next shelf in the display. Kensington had given him the whole of Sunday off, so after spending the morning doing some coursework, they'd decided to go for a wander about town and do some sightseeing. They'd ended up down by the waterfront and were killing time while they waited for the ferry over to Protection Island by browsing a souvenir shop.

"Whatever you want to tell me," Zach said, ignoring the trinkets around them, Drew his only focus. "I know she took over raising you when your parents died, but you haven't said much else about her."

Drew smiled fondly. "Harriett is amazing. She never wanted kids of her own, she thinks she's terrible with them, but she did alright by me. She's a very no-nonsense woman, but she's such a nice person. I mean, she can be sarcastic and hilarious but she's . . . kind. She'll drop everything to help anyone who needs it." He picked up a beanie and fiddled with the tag as he spoke. "She always told me she was never trying to replace my mom, but I hardly remember my mother. I remember her making me cinnamon buns, and I remember her staying up all night once when I was really sick with a fever. I remember little things like that, but I can't remember what her voice sounded like or what sort of clothes she liked to wear. I have photos of her and my dad, but I don't think I could pick them out of a police lineup, if that makes sense. So whether she meant to be or not, Aunt Harriett *is* my mom. She raised me, she gave up so much for me, and she loves me exactly as I am. I don't think my mom would mind that I see Harriett in her shoes now because she's done such an amazing job."

"What was your childhood like?" Zach prompted.

Drew shrugged. "I dunno, normal I guess? I don't really remember too much about my life before. I was just young, and I guess the trauma of losing my parents doesn't help. I can't even imagine how hard it was for Harriett. She'd just gotten back on her feet after getting out of a horrible relationship with some absolute asshole. He'd pretty much taken everything from her and left her with nothing. So here she is, slowly scraping her life back together, and she gets lumped with some kid she never wanted."

Zach frowned. "Did she ever say that to you?"

Shaking his head, Drew put the beanie down and moved on. "God, no. She came to Edmonton as soon as the social worker called to advise her of the accident, even though she couldn't afford the expense of a trip across the country. My parents didn't have much either, but what they did have paid for us to move my stuff over to Victoria and to buy the basics. Harriett didn't have much of a social life, but what she had now played second fiddle to taking care of me and picking up extra shifts at the hospital. Her wage barely covered her own living expenses, let alone another mouth to feed, but she never complained, never made me feel guilty."

"She does sound lovely," Zach said, wrapping an arm around Drew's waist as they left the store and started along the boardwalk toward the small ferry dock.

"She is. I honestly never realised how tough things were for us until I was much older. She hid it from me so well."

"How so?"

"God, there are so many ways. Okay, so take Christmas for example. We didn't have much at all and she could never afford to buy me huge gifts or anything, but she always made the occasion really special. Leading up to Christmas, we'd walk around the neighbourhood and look at all the lights, and we'd stay up late with mugs of hot chocolate and watch Christmas movies. We'd go to the dollar store and buy cheap decorations for the apartment, and if I was lucky, they'd have some discounted baking supplies and we'd make simple cookies. My gifts were normally homemade, like knitted scarves and beanies and gloves, or she'd make me a scavenger hunt and I'd have to find clues around the neighbourhood. They'd lead me back to the apartment where she'd hidden a toy she'd managed to save up for, and then we'd have lunch together. Christmas lunch was always really fancy, and I think that was because food pantries always get nicer donations during the holidays. There were always some treats, and I looked forward to it every year."

They joined the line for the ferry, squeezing into the floating waiting room and snagging the last two seats on the wooden benches inside. A man came around selling tickets, and Zach waved off Drew's offer to pay for them.

"Tell me more," Zach urged as they watched the tiny boat which would take them across to the island approach.

Drew thought for a moment, then said, "A couple of times, we didn't have enough money to pay the hydro bill, so we didn't have power for a few days. I never actually realised, because Harriett would tell me we were going to be doing 'living-room camping.' We'd make a tent out of all the blankets—essentially a blanket fort—and she'd string up these battery-operated fairy lights, and I had a Transformers flashlight I'd gotten for my birthday that I loved using. We'd play card games and make shadow puppets on the walls, and tell ghost stories. I was always so excited when we got to do living-room camping that I never questioned it. It was just too much fun."

"If I ever get the pleasure of meeting your aunt," Zach said, as the small boat bumped against the dock and the crew got it ready for the people coming from the island to depart. "I am going to lavish her with gifts and all the things she could ever need or desire. She deserves so much and more for being such a wonderful support to you."

Smiling, Drew squeezed his hand. "And I'd let you do that because she does deserve it. She deserves all the good things."

The tiny ferry emptied and those in the little waiting room were allowed to board. Being a warm summer's day and a Sunday to boot, the ferry was absolutely packed, and Drew and Zach squeezed into a space on the narrow bench seat. Zach lifted his arm and held Drew close, ostensibly to make more room for the couple who tried to fit in next to them without climbing right onto their laps, but mostly, Drew suspected, because he simply enjoyed being affectionate. He was constantly touching Drew, whether it be casual touches as he spoke, a guiding hand to the small of the back as they walked, or cuddling up close as they watched a movie before bed. Drew knew Zach was attracted to him, but the majority of his touches weren't sexual in nature. They were casual, performed without conscious thought, just simple acts of affection.

It made Drew feel all warm and fuzzy on the inside.

The ferry was soon motoring through the harbour towards Protection Island. Drew had been before, and although there wasn't much to *do* there, he had wanted to share it with Zach. Lunch at the pub and then a stroll around the island would be a relaxing way to spend the afternoon. He was still doing the homework Kensington had assigned him, locating his centre and making contact with his power in the middle of everyday activities. He figured now was as good a time as any to do so, and he reached down inside himself, pleased when he immediately felt the spark waiting for him. He gathered a small amount to him, not doing anything with it, just running his metaphorical fingers through it . . . connecting with it. Drew almost felt like he was getting it used to him, somehow. Like perhaps it was a stray cat and it would get spooked if he suddenly tried to snatch it up out of the blue one day. He took a few more moments to just *be* with the magic and then he let it go, letting it slip back into the well of power within him.

The sun was warm against his face, Zach was a solid presence by his side, the cool breeze whipped against his skin, and Drew relaxed back and simply enjoyed being in the moment. A few minutes later, they were docking at Protection Island and they patiently waited for their turn to disembark.

They headed straight for the Dinghy Dock Pub, since it would likely be at capacity this close to lunchtime, and managed to snag one of the last remaining booths. Drew was pretty sure it wasn't luck that got them the table but the charming smile Zach flashed at the waitress. She looked a little flushed as she walked away, and he couldn't blame her. Zach was looking particularly sexy today in slim-fit jeans, a tight white tee, and heavy military-style boots. Where Drew was sure his own hair looked like a bird's nest from the wind off the ocean, Zach's dark hair looked artfully tousled by the breeze. He'd shaved that morning but he already had a hint of stubble, and it made his plush lips look all the more kissable for it.

They both ordered fish and chips, and chatted while they ate, and Drew amused himself by using his magic to move the salt and pepper shakers around the table when he was sure no one would notice. They didn't linger once their meals were done, since it was very crowded and noisy in the pub, and they were soon climbing up the ramp from the dock and walking along the narrow laneways that snaked around the island.

"So, when will you see your aunt again?" Zach asked, harking back to the conversation they'd been having previously.

"I'm not sure," Drew admitted. "I do try and get back to Victoria to see her once a month or so, but it all depends on her work schedule and whether I can afford the bus ticket." He didn't mention he'd rather go without food for a few days in order to scrape together the money for the bus than disappoint his aunt. "I'm due to see her soon, but I guess it depends on everything happening here."

"How so?"

He shrugged. "Kensington is giving up a lot of his time to train me, so it would feel a little rude to make him work around my social life."

"I'm sure he won't begrudge you a family visit," Zach said.

"Maybe. I'll have to wait and see what her new roster looks like anyway, so it could be a moot point. She picks up a lot of nights and weekend work—the shifts no one else really wants—because they pay so much better." He glanced over at Zach. "Is there a reason you asked?"

Zach grinned. "I'm sure you've figured out I'm dying to meet her."

Laughing, Drew nodded. "Yeah, it's pretty obvious."

"Would you have a problem with me meeting her?"

He looked away, feeling a nervous flutter in his stomach. "How exactly would I introduce you?"

"How would you like to introduce me?" Zach countered.

Drew could feel himself blush. "I mean, I know we've been doing stuff together and we told my friends we're dating, but that was mostly to shut Edward up, wasn't it? I don't want to lie to my aunt."

Zach stopped mid-stride to give Drew a long look. He then glanced around, nodded when he saw what he was looking for, then took Drew's hand and towed him off the laneway and into a small grove of trees. He led him far enough away that they were out of sight of anyone walking past, so they had some semblance of privacy, and then guided Drew to sit on a large rock. Crouching down in front of him, Zach took both of his hands in his. "Sweetness, how do *you* see us?"

Drew shrugged and looked away, unable to meet Zach's glorious whiskey-coloured eyes.

He heard Zach sigh. "Let me guess. You think I'm just having some fun with you until you figure out how to break my bonds to Oberon and then I'll be off on my merry way without a backward glance?"

Drew winced. That . . . wasn't far off the mark. "Um, maybe?"

A hand cupped Drew's cheek and gently turned his face until he met Zach's gaze. "I'm sorry if I've given you that impression, sweetness. I didn't mean to confuse you."

"No need to apologise," Drew said, aiming for nonchalant and probably failing terribly. "Why would you stick around for a nobody like me?"

"You are *not* a nobody," Zach told him sternly.

Drew couldn't help it—he rolled his eyes. "God, yes I am, Zach! I'm just a broke uni student who accidentally summoned you. There's nothing special about me, not really."

"I beg to differ."

He snorted. "Why, because I have magic? Magic is just another skill, like being able to sing or being really good at cooking. It doesn't make me a better person, or smarter, or make us suddenly compatible. What do we even have in common? You're . . . fuck, I don't even *know* how old you are, and you've experienced things I can't even begin to fathom. We've been thrown together by a summoning spell, but when that's gone and you're not tethered to me anymore, what's left, Zach? What on earth is there about me that could make you wanna stick around?" He realised his cheeks were wet, and he swiped away a tear.

Zach's eyes closed, and he looked immeasurably sad. "Oh, sweetness. I want to go back in time and find every single person who ever made you feel like you're not good enough and rip them to shreds." His eyes snapped open with a fierce expression. "I have a feeling I'll need to start with that piece of shit, Edward." He leaned forward until their foreheads were touching and his breath ghosted over Drew's face as he said, "You are not only sweet and kind but so damn smart, and you make me laugh so much. Do you know how long it's been since I've laughed so freely? It is *not* your magic that makes me want you, Drew Phillips. It's everything about you that makes you, *you*. Yes, I'm older than dirt, and I've seen some shit, but I reckon we're still a better love story than *Twilight*."

That made Drew huff out a small laugh.

"I may be some crazy mix of angel and demon, but one of my powers is sadly not being able to see the future," Zach continued. "I want to be with you even after we break Oberon's hold on me and the tethering spell as well. Will we last the distance? I *hope* we will, but I don't know for sure. You might get sick of me. Who knows. But I'm willing to try if you are. I want to date you and get to know you better and see where this goes. So I'm asking you . . . Is that something you want as well?"

Another tear slipped down Drew's cheek and he sniffled a little but nodded, their foreheads rubbing together. "Yes, I want that more than anything."

"I'm glad we've got that settled," Zach said.

Drew tried to meet Zach's eyes but ended up going cross-eyed instead. He laughed and pulled back, but ducked in again, this time to press his lips to Zach's. "Thank you for being so patient with me."

"It's my pleasure," Zach assured him.

"I wish I had more experience with relationships so I wouldn't keep fucking up."

Fire flashed in Zach's eyes and he growled, deep and low in his chest. For an actual angel, he pulled off "demon" remarkably well. "I'm glad no one else has gotten to touch you but me," Zach gritted out. "Just the *thought* of someone else laying their hands on you . . ." He trailed off, and the fire dimmed then died out. He swallowed hard and closed his eyes. "Sweetness, you are *mine*. I know that's archaic and wrong on so many fucking levels, but I don't even want to think about you with someone else. I'm *glad* you don't have any experience because that means I'm your first in everything.

I'm the one who gets to show you pleasure beyond your wildest dreams. *I'm* the one who gets to experience everything with you. *I'm* the only one who gets to put their hands on you."

Drew chuckled and hugged Zach to him because he was being rather sweet, but he did give him a couple of condescending pats on the head as well because he was also being a possessive bastard. "Calm down, you big idiot, before those flames turn into glowing red flags. I've *not* been with anyone else, so there's no point getting your panties in a twist over shit that hasn't happened. Besides, it *wasn't* the sex stuff I was talking about. It's all the other stuff that goes with a relationship."

Zach managed to look contrite, which was a feat in itself. "Sorry," he mumbled.

"It's okay, but you'll have to reign that shit in if you ever want to get back into Heaven, you know. I don't think they like their angels being all fiery-eyed and growly."

"I told you, I've changed too much to ever go back. They'd never accept me after what I've had to do."

Zach looked sad again, and Drew silently cursed himself for bringing it up. He'd meant it as a joke, but clearly, it was *way* too soon for jokes. Drew cast his mind about for a way to cheer Zach up and felt a delicious thrill go through him as the perfect idea occurred to him. He motioned for Zach to get up off his knees, and then stood himself. He pushed Zach down until he was sitting on the rock where Drew had been, and then he sank to his knees.

"What are you doing, sweetness?" Zach asked, curious.

Drew gestured around them. "We seem to have found a quiet little corner of the island that's free of tourists. Since we won't make the next ferry back, we have at least an hour to kill. I thought now might be the perfect time to get some more *relationship experience*." He waggled his eyebrows in a manner he hoped looked suggestive and not just deranged.

Zach smirked as he caught on to what Drew was implying and he popped the button open on his jeans. "Why, Mr Phillips, I never thought you'd have a kink for public indecency."

"I figure I gotta try everything at least once," Drew shot back. He pulled the zipper down and leaned in close to add in a whisper, "But I have to say, *I* won't be the one with his dick out in public."

Zach grinned. "No, but you *will* be doing some *very* indecent things to me."

"True. Now, hurry up and get these jeans out of my way."

The trouble with skin-tight jeans, Drew learned, was that they were remarkably difficult to get out of in a hurry. They were too tight for Zach to simply roll them down his thighs, and when he pushed them down around his ankles, the rock he was sitting on was too pointy for his angelic ass. Eventually, he shucked the jeans entirely—after first having to undo his laces and take off his boots—and then he folded the jeans and placed them on the rock as a cushion of sorts.

It was an entire production.

"Are you just about done?" Drew asked archly.

Zach waved at his exposed junk in a regal manner. "All yours." It was unfair, Drew thought, just how sexy Zach looked at that moment. Anyone else who was sitting on a rock in just a T-shirt and socks would look ridiculous, but Zach looked like sex personified. Maybe it was the fact he was already hard in anticipation, and a drop of precum was already beading at the tip of his cock? Nonetheless, he was sexy as sin, and Drew wasn't going to waste another minute. He *needed* to taste him.

Leaning forward, Drew lapped at the head of Zach's cock. Salt and musk burst over his tongue and he found he rather liked the taste. He tongued at the slit again, hoping for more, and was rewarded with another drop of precum. He twirled his tongue around the head a few times, then sucked the tip into his mouth.

Above him, Zach moaned softly and combed his fingers through Drew's hair. "So good, sweetness."

Feeling a little more confident, he bobbed his head a little, taking more and more of Zach's cock into his mouth. Saliva dripped from his lips and ran down the outside of Zach's shaft, and Drew wrapped his hand around the base and used that to slick the way as he pumped him slowly. At one point, the head of Zach's cock nudged against the very back of his mouth, at the entrance of his throat, and he had to pull back as he coughed and gagged. Once he caught his breath, he tried again, and soon got comfortable with the idea of a cock being so deep in his mouth. He bobbed down even deeper, thinking maybe he could try and take it into his actual throat. He'd watched porn heaps of times and the recipient always seemed to enjoy deep throating, and he wanted Zach to get as much pleasure from this as he could.

Suddenly Zach hissed, and he gently pulled Drew off his cock.

"What is it? What did I do wrong?" Drew asked, worried.

"I got snagged on your teeth," Zach said, wincing.

Drew frowned and rubbed at his jaw, which was aching from being held open so wide. "I thought I was keeping them out of the way."

"Not your front teeth . . . your molars."

"Oh. Um. I don't think I can make them go any wider."

Zach huffed out a soft laugh. "Yeah, that's kind of physically impossible."

"So how do I deep throat you without hurting you?"

"Some positions can make it easier, like if you're on your back on the edge of a bed, but I don't think that'll help here, sweetness. I think your jaw is too small. I don't think I'll actually fit between your back teeth to get anywhere near your throat."

Feeling dejected, Drew sank down until he was sitting on his heels. "But how will I make you feel good?"

Zach cupped his cheek and stroked Drew's face with his thumb. "You already were. I don't need you to take me all the way down your throat to feel good."

"But everyone loves being deep throated!" Drew objected.

Zach shrugged. "It is good, but it's not the be-all and end-all of blowjobs, sweetness. I think a lot of it's more about how it looks than how it feels. Most of the nerve endings are around the head of my cock, so there's not quite as much stimulation when I'm being deep throated."

Drew's eyes narrowed. He suddenly understood Zach's flare of possessiveness earlier. He did *not* enjoy the thought of someone else deep throating his angel.

Zach caught the change of expression and hurried to add. "What you were doing felt amazing, Drew. I don't need anything more from you. If you don't like giving head, you don't have to do it at all."

"I *do* like it," Drew protested. "Apparently I just suck at it."

"Hey, none of that," Zach chided. "You're doing great. I wouldn't lie to you about something like this. It takes practice, but for your first time, I have absolutely no complaints, okay?"

"Okay," Drew agreed begrudgingly.

"Did you want to keep going? As I said, you don't have to."

Drew pushed himself back up to his knees. "Yes, I want to keep going. Just as long as it *does* feel good and you're not just saying it does to make me feel better."

"I swear, I won't lie to you, Drew," Zach vowed. "It really does feel amazing."

Feeling better, Drew bent his head back to the task, concentrating on the head and crown with his mouth and using his hand for the rest. He found that Zach was most vocal when he flicked his tongue against his frenulum and tongued at his slit. He did that as often as he could, loving the salty bursts he was rewarded with along with the pants and moans.

A few minutes later, Zach tried to urge him off once more. "I'm close," he gasped.

Drew shook him off and kept going. As much as he appreciated the offer, he loved the taste of Zach's precum and wanted to taste all of him. He hollowed his cheeks and sucked gently on the head, and Zach thrust shallowly into his mouth. The head of his cock was smooth and slick against Drew's tongue, and he was leaking constantly. Then Zach cried out and shuddered, and Drew's mouth was flooded with cum.

Oh. Oh, dear.

It wasn't the taste that was the problem, but the feel of it. Drew had always been sensitive to textures of foods, and having a mouth full of hot sticky cum was much, much worse than he'd anticipated. Zach was still pulsing over his tongue when Drew gagged and yanked himself off. He turned to the side and, much to his mortification, threw up the entire contents of his stomach onto the ground.

They must have looked a right sight—Zach, pantsless and panting, his spent cock laying against his T-shirt, and Drew, red-faced and on his knees, retching into the grass. He was going to die of embarrassment, he just knew it. Just as soon as he got his roiling stomach under control. He sighed internally. Those fish and chips had been *really* good. Pity they weren't anywhere near as nice on the way back up.

A hand settled on his back and rubbed soothing circles. "You okay?" Zach asked once Drew had gone an entire thirty seconds without barfing.

"Oh my God, I am *so* sorry," Drew cried, unable to even look at Zach.

"Hey, it's okay, I swear. Come here," Zach urged and pulled him up into his lap. He'd not gotten dressed again as yet and Drew kept his eyes down, looking at the contrast between the hair on Zach's thighs and the denim of his own jeans.

To make matters even worse, Drew felt his throat begin to burn and tears sting at his eyes. For fuck's sake, hadn't he cried enough for one day? If he didn't already, Zach was going to think he really was a loser now.

"Sweetness, please don't be upset," Zach soothed, holding him close.

"I'm so embarrassed," Drew half wailed, turning and burying his face against his angel's chest.

"Don't be. It was your first time. It's a learning curve, okay? You'll learn what you like and what you don't, and next time will be even better."

"Next time? You really want there to be a next time when blowing you caused me to throw up?"

"Of course I do, but only if you want to try again. BJs aren't for everyone."

"I was so looking forward to it," Drew told him. "I can't believe I'm such a loser."

"You're not, and I won't have you saying things like that about yourself. Real life isn't like porn or romance novels. Not everyone likes to swallow. Hell, a lot of people don't like giving head at all, or if they do, they use it as foreplay and don't continue until climax. There is *nothing* wrong with you." He pressed a kiss to Drew's temple. "You made me feel so good, and I'm the one who's sorry it made you sick."

"I just wanted it to be perfect."

"And it *was*, because it was you and me," Zach assured him. "Please don't be upset."

Drew sighed and settled himself even closer against Zach's chest. He was feeling slightly better about the whole thing, so long as he didn't look over to the right and see the puddle of vomit on the ground. Ew, were those carrots? When had he eaten carrots? He didn't remember those . . .

After a few minutes, they heard voices nearby, and they were both jolted back to the reality of the situation. Yes, they were off the laneways, but they were still in a public place, and Zach was still half naked.

"I guess I should get dressed," Zach said, giving Drew one more squeeze before he climbed off his lap.

"Probably for the best," Drew agreed.

As Zach dressed, they both went to great pains to ignore the soggy return of Drew's lunch, which was beginning to attract a colony of ants. Zach took Drew's hand in his and led the way through the grove of trees and back to the laneway. "I suppose we should be heading back to the dock," he said.

Drew nodded. "Yeah, the ferry will be here soon." He paused and then sighed. "I really am sorry. It's not how I wanted that to go."

"I know it's not, but it really is alright. When we get home, you can have a warm shower, we can order some takeout, and have a nice relaxing evening. Maybe I can even return the favour if you're up for it?"

Drew gave him a wry smile. "I don't think that'll be a problem. I'm always up for your mouth on me."

Zach grinned and leaned in to kiss him, but then pulled back at the last second and kissed his cheek instead.

"Urgh, yeah, sorry about that," Drew said with a wince. "I wonder if anyone waiting for the ferry will have a mint on them?"

Oops, I Did It Again

"So, Drew, how are things going with that hunk of yours?" Dom asked as they were packing up from their study session.

Drew grinned as he thought of Zach and everything they'd been doing lately. They'd still not had penetrative sex as yet, but over the past several weeks they'd gotten each other off almost every night. Drew was even getting pretty good at blow jobs now and hadn't barfed since that memorable first time. He knew he'd be ready to take that final step soon, but he wanted to be in the right headspace for it. At the moment, he was being torn between his university studies, his magical studies, and his Zach studies, and he wanted to be able to concentrate one hundred percent when the time came that they actually made love. As Zach kept assuring him, there was no rush and they could take their time.

Gwen reached over and pulled down the collar of Drew's polo shirt, and smirked at the large hickey on his throat. "I'd say things are going pretty good," she teased.

A white and brown paw with claws extended swiped at her, and she yanked her hand away, glaring at the cat who had leaped out of the backpack. Zach jumped into Drew's arms, purring loudly, and rubbed his furry cheek against his. "Sorry," Drew apologised. "But you know how Noodle is."

Gwen shook her head, sending her blonde ponytail swinging. "Your cat is *weird*, Drew. I've never seen a cat so fucking *possessive* of their owner before. If anyone so much as touches you, he goes into attack mode."

Zach purred even louder.

"What can I say? He doesn't like sharing."

No, I do not, Zach agreed silently.

"How is he with Zach?" Dom asked.

"Oh, he adores him," Drew said, trying not to laugh out loud at the ridiculousness of having a conversation about Zach's different forms with people who had no clue.

"That's lucky, I guess," Dom said. "Might be awkward otherwise, what with all of that bare skin within scratching distance." He held a hand out to Zach, allowing him to sniff his knuckles, and then Zach tilted his head, permitting Dom to scritch at his neck. He was the only one of Drew's friends who Zach allowed to pet him in his cat form, and it always made Dom's dark eyes light up when he was allowed.

"So, who's up for getting a coffee?" Gwen asked the group as she finished zipping up her bag.

"Sorry, I can't," Drew said. "I have plans for tonight and I gotta go to the grocery store first."

"Ooh, romantic night in?" Dom asked.

Drew grinned. "Yep! Zach's been so good to me, always cooking and taking care of me, so I figured tonight I'd try to return the favour."

You know you don't have to, Zach told him.

I know, but I want to, Drew thought back at him.

"Have fun," Dom said, giving Zach one last scritch. "We'll see you tomorrow."

Drew held the backpack open for Zach but he refused to jump in, instead scooting further up Drew until he was draped over his chest and shoulder. "Oh, I see how it is. You want to be carried, huh?"

Zach purred again and nuzzled his cold cat nose against Drew's cheek.

"Okay guys, see ya!" He headed off, his backpack on one shoulder and his other hand cradling Zach's butt to keep him steady. The weather had turned cool, and the wind had a chill to it so it was nice having a small warm body against his throat.

You're better than a scarf, Drew told Zach.

I don't like it when you're cold, sweetness. There was a pause. *You really don't have to go to any trouble and cook for me. It's okay. Really.*

Drew frowned. *Wait a second . . . You don't want to eat my food because you think I'm a terrible cook. That's it, isn't it?*

The silence was incriminating.

I'm not that *bad!* Drew protested.

Drew, Zach said gently. *The last time you tried cooking something more than just pasta and sauce, you summoned a demon.*

That was an accident!

I'm just saying, we can always just order in.

More determined than ever, Drew headed towards the Country Grocer which was next to the bus stop. *It'll be different this time, Zach. I'm doing well in my lessons, and I've got control of my magic. It'll be fine, you'll see.*

It wasn't fine.

Drew looked up at the two demons in his kitchen—*real* demons this time. He froze. They looked human, but there was a red glow to their eyes and the smaller one had a mean smile on his lips. He was wiry and powerful looking, with oily blond hair that hung limply around his shoulders. "Well, well, well, look what we have here," he sneered, his eyes trailing over Drew as a forked tongue came out to lick at his lips. "Looks like Zachariel has his own little plaything."

The other demon nodded his agreement. "Very pretty. I'm gonna enjoy tearing him apart." And he certainly looked like he could tear Drew apart. He was tall and muscular, and a scar marred the dark skin of one cheek.

"Now, now, Asmodeus, there's no rush," the first demon said silkily. "Let's have a little fun first. You know lust is my favourite cardinal sin." He took a step towards Drew, which finally broke him from his frozen state.

"Zach!" Drew cried, edging away from the demons and backing himself up against the sink.

"Drew, what's wrong?" Zach called from the other room—where Drew had made him stay, on the very edge of the ten-foot limit so dinner could be a surprise—a note of worry in his voice. He appeared in the doorway and his eyes narrowed as he took in the scene. "Beelzebub, Asmodeus, what are you doing here?" he all but snarled.

"Oh, we were *summoned*, Zachariel," the one called Beelzebub said. He smiled wickedly and tilted his head in Drew's direction. "Looks like your little plaything here isn't getting what he needs from you, so he called for some *real* demons to give him what he needs." Beelzebub looked back at Drew and his forked tongue licked over his bottom lip again. It was more than a little creepy. "It's going to be utterly *delicious* destroying something so sweet."

Zach growled and lunged at Beelzebub, but Asmodeus stepped in between them and stopped Zach with a hand to his chest. "Now, now, Zachariel," Asmodeus said in a low, menacing voice. "If you don't behave, your toy is gonna suffer more than he needs to."

Zach narrowed his eyes and took a step back, seemingly in retreat, but as soon as Asmodeus dropped his guard, Zach struck, punching Asmodeus across the jaw and then using the distraction to cross the kitchen and plant himself in front of Drew. "You won't be laying a finger on Drew," he told the two demons. "He's under *my* protection." Asmodeus wiped his nose, glancing down at the smear of blood on his hand then back up at Zach. "Your protection, huh? How much good is that gonna do the kid?"

"You're the one bleeding," Drew snapped, feeling brave enough to be snarky now he had Zach by his side. "I reckon it's worth a bit."

Asmodeus sneered at Drew. "He took me by surprise, that's all. Your cunt of an angel ain't got nothin' on me."

"Charming as usual, I see," Zach drawled.

Asmodeus gave a feral grin in reply.

"This is all well and good," Beelzebub announced, looking rather bored. "But I'd much rather get to the fun part of this evening."

"Oh? And what does that entail?" Zach asked.

"Well, *obviously* it'll be us disposing of you and then having our wicked way with your young Drew here." The calculated smile he flashed Drew made his blood run colder than Asmodeus's evil bluster had.

Drew noticed that every muscle in Zach's back had gone tense and he was practically vibrating with potential violence. "And I told you, neither of you will lay a hand on him," Zach reiterated. "Now fuck off back to where you came from before this gets any worse for you than it already is."

Beelzebub shook his head, making a condescending *tsk* noise. "My dear, dear Zachariel, how naive of you. This isn't a *social* call; we've been summoned! Your precious Drew can send us back anytime he desires." He glanced behind Zach to Drew, who couldn't quite maintain eye contact with the demon's red eyes. "So go on then, precious one. Send us back." He paused and cocked his head to one side. "Oh, wait! I'm guessing if you *could have*, you *would have* by now." He held a hand up to his face in theatrical surprise and turned to Asmodeus. "Oh dear! I don't think he can!"

Asmodeus grinned again, his forked tongue peeking out between his teeth. "Seems like. That's a real shame. Guess we're welcome after all."

"Yes, we're not going *anywhere* in a hurry," Beelzebub added.

Zach made the low growling noise again, and the hairs on the back of Drew's neck stood up. "He might not be able to *send* you back to Hell," he told them. "But that doesn't mean I can't *kill* you. The proper death . . . the one there's no coming back from."

Drew didn't understand, but it was a threat the two demons didn't take lightly.

"Now, now, Zachariel," Beelzebub cautioned. "That threat applies to you as well."

Zach dropped into a crouch and snarled, "Bring it!" before leaping towards them.

Drew stumbled back as the two demons and one angel began to brawl, falling this way and that across the small kitchen, smashing into the table and bench top, sending plates and dishes smashing to the floor. For a moment it looked like Zach had the upper hand, but Drew knew that being outnumbered as he was, it wouldn't last long. Zach had never divulged what would happen if he got seriously hurt, but from the sounds of it he could die just as easily as a human could . . . without the afterlife waiting for him. A chill seeped into Drew's blood at the mere thought of losing Zach, and he knew he had to do something, *anything*, to help.

Trying to focus and find his centre like Kensington had taught him, Drew searched for the spark of power which resided inside him. He'd been able to tap into it to do small things during his training so far, but he knew there was a vast amount of power lurking within. He just needed to reach inside and draw on it.

The fear he felt helped . . . the desperate need to help Zach, to keep him safe. Suddenly, Drew was overcome with an almost blinding rush of power. He took a deep breath, trying to control the magic which surged through him as he looked at the fight happening mere feet away, dismissing Zach and focusing on the two demons. He had no spell, no incantation to recite, and no handy phrase in Latin to use, but he concentrated all of his willpower on what he wanted to happen, hoping it would be enough, that it would act as a guide for his magic. "*BEGONE!*" he thundered, causing the walls to shake and more dishes to rattle off the bench and smash upon the floor. There was a bright flash, and then with a loud *crack,* the two demons were gone and only he and Zach remained.

A beam of blinding light appeared in the centre of the kitchen, and when it disappeared Kensington was there in its place in his long forest-green robes. He looked around the room, taking in Drew's shaken appearance and Zach's bloody nose, and arched one of his brows. "What on earth happened here?" he asked.

Worship

"Drew could have been hurt!" Zach snapped at Kensington, brushing aside the ice pack Drew was holding out to him. "Where the hell were you?"

Kensington had righted one of the kitchen chairs and was sitting in it, looking scarily at home amidst the wreckage of the kitchen. "I *had* been dealing with another matter," he said archly. "I actually have a *job* to do, you know. I don't exist solely to babysit Mr Phillips."

"Hey!" Drew protested.

"He could have been hurt!" Zach reiterated, pacing the room in his agitation.

"Zach, I'm fine," Drew assured him. "It's okay."

Zach sighed and finally stilled, pinching the bridge of his nose. "I know. It's just, it could have gone very differently."

"At least they seem to be gone for good," Kensington said.

"Did I . . . did I *kill* them?" Drew asked, not sure if he wanted to know the answer. Demons or not, he didn't really want murder on his hands.

"It's hard to say," Kensington said. "There's no trace of their energy remaining here at all, but that could just be because you banished them and sealed off any chance of them returning."

"Trust me, Drew, the universe is a better place if you did," Zach said. "No one's gonna miss them."

That really didn't make Drew feel any better. He resisted the sudden urge to cry, but he couldn't stop the tears from welling in his eyes.

Zach must have seen it because all the anger and tension drained from him at once and he hurried across the kitchen to Drew, and took him gently by the arms. "Hey, sweetness, it's okay."

"But I might have killed them," Drew said, his voice trembling.

"Fuck, I'm sorry, Drew. I'm so sorry you were put in this situation because of me." He pulled Drew to his chest and wrapped his arms around him, and Drew buried his face against Zach's shirt.

"It's my fault, not yours," Drew told him. "It was *me* who stupidly thought I could make dinner. If I'd just listened to you and ordered in, this would never have happened."

Kensington stood up and laid a hand on Drew's shoulder. "Honestly, Drew, there's no proof that you *did* kill them. You may very well have simply banished them. Don't be too hard on yourself."

Drew nodded but didn't look up.

"Why don't you come round tomorrow and we'll unpack exactly what you did and see if we can figure out what happened?"

"Okay," Drew whispered.

"Good, then I'll see you both then."

Drew stayed where he was but he felt the pressure in the room change, and then when it had returned to normal, he knew Kensington was gone, having magically transported himself back to the Collective. He nuzzled against Zach's chest, taking comfort in his warmth. "I'm sorry," he said, voice muffled against the fine material of his shirt.

"What on earth are *you* sorry for?" Zach asked, sounding surprised.

Drew shrugged. "For getting upset, like a baby."

"Oh, sweetness, no. Don't apologise for being *human*. You have every right to be upset."

Drew slipped his arms further around Zach to hug him tighter and felt how tense he was. "You're still upset too."

Zach sighed. "Yeah, Drew, I am."

"Why?"

"Because Beelzebub and Asmodeus could really have hurt you, and I would never have forgiven myself if they had."

"But they didn't."

"But they *could have*. I know I'm being silly, but dammit, Drew, I should be protecting you. I didn't do a very good job."

Drew had been going to wait until after their romantic dinner to attempt to take their relationship to the next level, but he figured now was as good a time as any. "Zach, I'm fine, I promise. But maybe it would help you calm down if you could see for yourself? Get up close and personal."

"What do you mean?"

Drew's cheeks were so hot, he was sure his face was on fire. "I um . . . I want you to . . . "

"Yes?" Zach urged.

"I want you to fuck me," Drew blurted.

Zach grinned, and it was good to see him loosening up, even if the cost was Drew's dignity. "Oh really?"

Drew nodded. "Yeah."

"And you think this will help calm me down?"

He nodded again. "Yep."

Zach reached up and brushed his thumb across Drew's cheek. "You know, I think you're right."

Drew leaned into the touch and his eyes fluttered closed. "What do you need me to do?" he asked.

"You don't have to do a thing, sweetness, just let me take care of you," Zach whispered, then he scooped Drew into his arms and walked through to the main room so he could put him gently on the bed.

Drew tried to calm his nerves as Zach divested him of his clothing, peppering his skin with kisses as it was revealed. He could do this, he could. He *wanted* this. There was *nothing* to be nervous about. Zach was going to take care of him.

And his angel did.

Once they were both naked, Zach took his time, caressing and kissing all over Drew's body. His strong fingers danced over every curve, each muscle, each protruding bone. It wasn't long before Drew's whole body relaxed and he sank against the mattress, his eyes closed as he simply allowed himself to feel. "You're so beautiful," Zach whispered. "You look like more of an angel than I ever did." Then he captured Drew's mouth in a kiss which was both gentle and needy.

Drew didn't even hear Zach get supplies, but shortly afterwards his legs were being encouraged to part and he felt the bed shift as Zach settled between them. He felt a finger circle his entrance and a moment later it was back, slick with lube. As it sank inside, Drew felt a momentary pang of panic at the intrusion—it felt *massive* and it was only a fingertip!—but Zach paused, ran his other hand soothingly over Drew's side, and then as his body relaxed once more, it suddenly didn't feel big and scary anymore, but simply not enough.

More? Zach's voice whispered in Drew's mind as if he didn't want speech to intrude upon their intimacy.

Yes!

Zach slipped the finger in even deeper and then pulled out slightly before slipping it back in. He repeated this slowly a few times, but at Drew's inarticulate whine for more, he began to fuck into him even faster.

More, Zach, please, Drew begged silently.

The single digit was removed, but was soon back with another, wet and cool with more lube. There was a slight burn as the wider girth breached him, but it soon passed and Drew bucked his hips, taking Zach in even deeper. Zach chuckled and then twisted his fingers around, searching for something. Everything suddenly felt even better, and Drew knew Zach had found his prostate. It wasn't electric, and it didn't make him want to instantly come like he'd seen in porn. It was simply more pleasurable. The more Zach slid the pads of his fingers across the spot, the better it felt, the feeling building slowly and gradually. Drew's cock was lying hard against his stomach, forgotten for now but dripping constantly.

I want you so much, sweetness.

Please, Zach, need you inside me.

Zach withdrew his fingers, and Drew let his eyes flutter open so he could watch Zach slick up his cock. Zach caught him watching and smiled, a smile full of fondness and affection, and Drew smiled back. His heart felt so full he was worried it might burst. Was this love? Or was it simply lust? He didn't know and now wasn't the time to ponder such things, so instead he drew Zach down into another kiss, eager for more.

Zach gazed down at Drew beneath him and was momentarily floored by how deep his feelings were for him. Trusting, kind, and funny, Drew had brought joy and laughter back into Zach's life. He had a fierce need to protect Drew, to keep him safe, to make him happy, and his heart clenched as he remembered how close he'd come to losing him that day. Beelzebub and Asmodeus had been dangerous, and they would have torn Drew apart if it meant making Zach suffer. When Drew had banished them—more than likely killing them in the process, but he'd keep that tidbit to himself as he knew it would upset Drew—he'd felt immense relief. The threat was gone and Drew would be safe.

Zach had been unable to stop himself from touching every inch of Drew's skin, caressing it with his lips and checking for hidden injuries with his hands. He'd known deep down that Drew was fine, but he'd had to check, to make sure just in case. But Drew was unharmed, and he was perfect, and he wanted Zach. Zach understood just how big a deal this was for Drew, and he was going to do everything he could to make this the most glorious moment of Drew's life.

When he finally slipped inside Drew, so tight and hot, he watched intently for any signs of distress. Drew had closed his eyes again but his face was slack with pleasure, his mouth open in a soft O. Zach sank in slowly . . . slowly . . . taking his time, giving Drew time to get used to the feeling of being filled with more than just fingers. When he finally felt his pelvis pushing snugly against Drew's ass, he leaned down and slipped his arm under his shoulders, holding him close as he balanced on his other elbow. *Feel so good,* he whispered inside Drew's mind.

I never thought it would be like this, Drew replied.

I'm gonna take care of you, Drew. I'll make you feel so good.

He felt Drew's lips move in a smile against his cheek, and Zach held him even tighter. When Drew's hips began to rock, Zach started to move—shallow thrusts because of the way they were entwined, but he knew he was putting pressure on Drew's prostate the whole time.

Zach had never had sex with anyone like this before. He'd never cared about anyone like this before either. He knew what they were doing wasn't having sex, or fucking, or any of the other vulgar terms that were used . . . they were making love. And as he kissed Drew deeply, moving slowly inside him, he knew it wasn't just a saying. He loved Drew, even though they'd only known each other for such a short time. He buried his face against Drew's throat, holding him even closer as he continued to move inside him.

Suddenly there was a weight on his back he hadn't felt in centuries, and he gasped, causing Drew's eyes to fly open. He looked up in wonder as Zach exercised muscles he'd long thought lost. Black feathers with a faint red sheen to them dipped down to caress Drew's face.

"Oh, Zach," he said aloud. "They're beautiful. Just like you."

Zach couldn't say anything as he found himself at a loss for words, so he tried to show Drew through actions. His wings blanketed them as they continued to make love, and they quivered as he came deep inside Drew. When Drew cried out as Zach jerked him to completion, they stroked lovingly over his cheek. He wrapped them both up in a feathery cocoon as they drifted off to sleep, and when he woke in the morning to find his wings were once again gone, he didn't despair. They had come back, the strength of his love for Drew giving them the life force they needed to exist. And he knew, without a doubt, that once the gem in his chest was gone, when his ties to Hell were cut, his wings would return.

Zach curled around Drew, holding him close, and allowed himself to drift back to sleep, content in the knowledge that things were going to be okay.

Werecat

Drew yawned, wanting nothing more than to call it a night, but he couldn't. He had an assignment due by the end of the week, and with his magical studies taking up most of his spare time, he'd fallen behind on his coursework. He'd begged off his lesson that evening with Kensington and had come straight to the library after class, determined to finish what he had to.

Zach was curled up on his lap in his cat form, his eyes closed and a soft purr emanating from him as he kneaded Drew's thigh. Every now and then, Drew would scritch the top of his head, and Zach would purr even louder. It always made Drew smile, and he was happy he could make Zach feel good, even when he was being forced to sit around and do nothing while Drew studied. He was just lucky there were very few people in the library and so no one had complained about him having a cat with him.

He managed to get another few paragraphs written and had almost finished when someone approached the table. Drew looked up and blanched when he saw it was Edward. He'd been even more snarky and horrible to Drew since the night at the club, but Drew had done his best to ignore him.

"Phillips," Edward said and sat down uninvited opposite Drew.

"Edward, to what do I owe the pleasure?" Drew asked coolly.

"What are you doing here so late?" Edward asked instead of answering. He was wearing a preppy sweater with dark blue designer pants, and his blond hair was carefully styled.

Drew tapped his laptop with his finger. "The assignment for Henderson."

Edward grunted, but didn't say anything in reply. Drew was usually so busy ignoring Edward that he didn't really ever look at him, so he was surprised to see Edward looked tired, with dark bags under his eyes. If it were anyone else, he might even be concerned, but as this was his long-time bully, Drew found he didn't feel much sympathy.

The silence drew out, becoming awkward and uncomfortable, but Drew was determined not to be the one who broke it. Edward had approached him for a reason and he could either spit it out or fuck off.

What do you think he wants? Zach asked silently.

No idea.

If he's an ass to you, I might have to scratch him up a little.

As much as I appreciate the sentiment, don't do anything that draws attention to you. I don't want the librarians to ban you from coming in here.

Hmph.

Drew continued to stare at Edward but arched his brows—both of them, since he didn't possess the skill to only lift one like Zach and Kensington, much to his annoyance. It seemed to be enough to jolt Edward from whatever fugue state he'd fallen into. "So, um, how have you been?" Edward finally asked.

Drew snorted. "Oh, great, you know, except for this dick who takes an unhealthy delight in making my life a misery." Seriously, who the hell did he think he was?

Edward managed to look chagrined. "Um, yeah, about that . . ." He ran a hand through his hair, and despite staring intently at Drew for the past five minutes, was suddenly unable to look him in the eye. "I'm sorry for being a douche. I hope you can forgive me."

Drew fought the urge to laugh in his face. "Are you serious right now? You make my life a living hell, not just in high school but at uni too, and you think one *I'm sorry* is enough to gain my forgiveness?"

You tell him, Drew! Zach said, sounding proud.

Edward winced. "I get it, okay. If I were in your shoes, I wouldn't be too quick to forgive me either, but I really hope we can put this aside so we can move on."

"Move on? Edward, I hate to break it to you, but we're not, and never will be, friends," Drew told him bluntly. "If you'd shown some form of maturity after high school, then maybe we could have been, but you didn't. You kept on being the same bully you've always been."

A flush spread over Edward's cheeks. "I was kinda hoping that maybe we could be *more* than friends."

Drew was rendered speechless, but Zach wasn't. *I'm* right *here! Who does he think he is?*

"Excuse me?" Drew finally managed to choke out.

"Phillips . . . I mean, *Drew*. I was hoping maybe we could get a coffee or something," Edward said, eventually meeting Drew's gaze.

"Even if you *hadn't* been a dick to me for the past six years of my life, you do remember Zach, yeah?" Drew held a hand up. "Really good-looking guy with a killer smile and an even better ass who I *happen* to be involved with? I'm pretty sure you can't have forgotten about him *that* quickly."

Instead of looking abashed, like Drew had expected him to for being called out, Edward became very earnest. "Look, I just really don't think he's right for you, Drew. He's gotta be at least twice your age, maybe even more. What can you possibly have in common with him?"

"More than you think," Drew snapped.

Edward shook his head. "There's just no way you can connect with someone that much older than you. *Really* connect."

"And you think I can connect with you? *Really* connect?" Drew threw his words back at him, and then his tone turned faux jovial. *"Oh, Edward, remember that time you damaged the lock on my locker so I couldn't hand in my essay on time, which was worth ten percent of my grade? Wasn't that* hilarious? *Oh, and what about the time you shoved me in the back so I tripped over the janitor's mop bucket and ripped open the knees of my only pair of jeans? We're so connected! It's enough to make me want to grow old with you!"* Drew batted his lashes at Edward and then an instant later dropped the facade and glared at him. "Trust me, I have much more of a connection with the man who treats me with respect, who cares about me, makes sure I'm looked after, and who can make me laugh. That will never be you."

Edward shook his head. "You're wrong, Drew," he insisted. "I *can* be that person for you."

"Years of teasing and bullying say otherwise."

"Did your mother never tell you that boys tease the people they like?"

"My mother is dead, Edward, so no, she didn't. My aunt, on the other hand, taught me that bullying is wrong, and that excusing that sort of behaviour as being okay because someone 'likes you' is *not* okay."

Edward was clearly getting frustrated now at his inability to convince Drew. There was nothing that could have prepared Drew for what he did next, though. Edward reached across the table, grabbed a handful of Drew's shirt, and hauled him into a kiss.

The action dislodged Zach from Drew's lap, and the angel was *not* happy with Edward's action. He hit the ground and transformed into his human form, upending the table and flipping it to one side. Zach roared as he pushed Edward away and inserted himself between him and Drew.

"What the fuck?" Edward cried as he fell onto his ass, staring up in horror at Zach. "Where did *you* come from?"

"How *dare* you touch Drew without his consent!" Zach snapped, and Drew could just imagine the look on his face. He couldn't *see* it, though, since Zach's back was pressed right up against his front.

"How did you do that?" Edward said, stuck on trying to figure out where Zach had come from. "You just appeared out of nowhere, man!"

"Do not concern yourself with where I came from," Zach said in a deadly voice. "Just remember that if you ever lay a finger on Drew again, I'll be there, and I won't let you walk away unscathed."

As menacing as Zach was being—Drew figured he'd had to perfect his acting ability after masquerading as a demon for centuries—Edward just really wasn't getting it, too caught up in where Zach had appeared from. He was looking around wildly, and then his eyes opened comically wide. "The cat! The cat is gone and you're here instead. Fuck, fuck, fuck. You're a . . . a . . . a *werecat!*"

This made Zach pause, and Drew placed a hand on his hip as he peered around his avenging angel at Edward on the ground. "What the hell?" Zach asked. "Werecat? What the fuck are you on about?"

Edward's eyes darted from side to side, his face pale with fear. "Does that mean werewolves exist as well? Oh, God, do you prowl around at the full moon, finding people to turn?" He audibly gulped. "D . . . D . . . Drew, are *you* a were creature as well?"

It was mean, but Drew wanted to laugh at the panic on Edward's face. Instead, he managed to school his expression into something almost blank and said, "I think it's time for you to go, Edward." He glanced over at the large window not far away. "The moon's getting pretty full, and I'm starting to feel peckish."

Edward yelped and scrambled to his feet, and with one last terrified glance at Drew and Zach, he ran off through the library. In the distance, Drew could hear a librarian scolding him for running, and then he was overcome with a fit of giggles. "W . . . w . . . werecat!" he laughed. "He thought you were a werecat!"

Zach snorted and turned, and pulled Drew against him. "Fucking moron."

Drew laughed some more as he tried to imagine what it must have looked like to someone who didn't know of Zach's capabilities. He really couldn't fault Edward for coming to that conclusion. He was distracted, though, by Zach's thumb coming up to wipe over his bottom lip. "What is it?" he asked, as he noted the intensity of Zach's gaze.

"You still have his saliva on you," Zach growled.

"Eww, yuck!" Drew wiped over his mouth with the back of his hand, trying to get rid of every last trace of the unwanted kiss. "Is it gone?"

"Yes," Zach said, but he still didn't look happy.

"You know what would make it better?" Drew asked.

"What?"

"If you got *your* saliva all over me instead."

Zach arched a brow. "Is that a really weird and disgusting way of saying you want me to kiss you?"

Drew laughed again. "Yeah, yeah it is." His voice turned as smouldering as he could make it. "I want you to claim me, Zach. Mark me as your own."

Zach's eyes went dark with lust and possession, and he threaded his fingers into the hair at the nape of Drew's neck, pulling their faces close together. "Now *that* I can do," he purred, then he proceeded to claim Drew right there in the library.

Angel Nip

Drew pursed his lips as he looked around his tiny apartment, doing the math in his head. Zach was lounging on the bed, scrolling through a news article on Drew's phone, and he cocked his head to one side when he noticed the frown. "What's up?" he asked.

"I'm trying to figure out where there'll be enough space for Dom and me to study," he mused. After the incident with Edward last week, Drew hadn't been comfortable attending the group study sessions any longer, and Dom had offered to study with him at a different time. Drew had jumped at the chance and had offered to have Dom over to his place, but as he looked around now, he worried there wouldn't be enough room.

"The kitchen?" Zach suggested.

"Hmmm, I guess." His little table *did* seat two people, but the chances of them fitting their laptops and textbooks on it were slim. "I suppose we can give it a go. If it doesn't work, I suppose we can move to the bed."

Zach was up and off the bed in a blink, crowding into Drew's personal space and literally growling. "*No one* gets to be on your bed with you but *me.*"

Drew's lips quirked as he looked up into Zach's fierce eyes. "Are most angels this possessive? Doesn't really feel like it's an angelic trait," he teased.

Zach wrapped his arms around Drew and nuzzled against his throat. "You're forgetting I spent centuries in Hell, sweetness. Some of their bad habits were bound to rub off on me."

Drew rubbed soothing circles on Zach's back. "And I get that, but I'm not a possession, Zach. Let me ask you this . . . Do you trust me?"

He nodded, his hair brushing the underside of Drew's chin tickling. "Of course I do."

"Then you know I'm not going to do anything with anyone other than you. Besides, you *like* Dom. He's a good guy."

"I know," Zach said, and it sounded suspiciously like a whine. "I just don't want him on your bed is all."

"Fine, I respect that," Drew assured him. "We'll keep it in the kitchen and if we need more room, I'll move to the floor."

"You can always sit on my lap," Zach offered.

He shook his head. "Other than not exactly solving the space problem, I won't be able to because *you* will be in your cat form."

Zach pulled back and looked incredulously at him. "I beg your pardon?"

"Ah, there are those angelic manners!" he teased. Zach reached around and smacked Drew's bottom, making him yelp. "Hey!"

"No sassing me, mister," Zach told him

"You *like* me sassing you."

"Fine, I can't deny that, but that's totally not the point here. Now, what the hell do you mean?"

Drew rolled his eyes and waved his hands in front of Zach. "This, all of this, just now! *That's* why you'll be in your cat form! You can be as possessive as you like as Noodle. Lay all over me, mark me as yours, glare at Dom all you like—that's acceptable as a cat but *not* as my boyfriend. Ergo, you will be a cat."

Zach pouted, which was both adorable and slightly ridiculous on a grown man, but he didn't argue. "Fine, but I expect belly rubs."

Drew leaned up on his tiptoes and pressed a kiss to the tip of Zach's nose. "You can have *all* the belly rubs."

The buzzer was soon ringing, indicating Dom had arrived, and Drew let him in, giving directions to his apartment. Zach pulled Drew in for one last kiss and then fluidly melted into Noodle. He leaped up into Drew's arms and twisted around onto his back, exposing his furry tummy. "You are so spoiled," Drew murmured as he stroked Zach softly. There was a knock on the door and Drew went over and opened it for Dom. "Hi," he said, standing aside to let him in.

"Hey," Dom said, and his eyes went soft when they landed on Zach. "And hello to you, Mr Noodle," he cooed and joined in with the belly rubs.

Drew could tell Zach was fighting it, but his cat instinct soon took over and he began to purr loudly, making Drew chuckle. *You're such a softie,* he said.

Less talking, more petting, Zach instructed.

Drew led Dom across the tiny main room and into the even smaller kitchen, suddenly feeling embarrassed. "Um, sorry. It's not as nice as your place," he apologised.

Dom gave him a funny look. "It's fine, Drew. There's no need to apologise." His look then turned serious. "How are you doing?"

Drew shrugged. "I'm okay, really. I appreciate you coming round here so I didn't have to see him."

Dom shook his head. "I can't believe he was such a dick!" He grimaced. "Actually, no, I can *totally* see him being such a dick, but still. Hitting on someone who's in a relationship is low. If it wasn't for the fact that Gwen and I have been grouped with him for Professor Coultard's assignment, I'd have booted him from the study group altogether."

"It's okay. I don't expect everyone else to stop being friends with him because of what he did."

Dom scowled. "Decent people would. As soon as this assignment is done and dusted, I don't want anything else to do with him."

"Has he, uh, said anything about it to you guys?" Drew asked, pretty sure Edward wouldn't say anything to anyone else about the conclusion he'd drawn, but needing to be sure.

Dom shook his head. "Nah, he's hardly said boo. He's acting really weird, though . . . jumpy at everything. Like, the other day we were heading to the coffee shop after the session and a woman was walking her dog across campus. He actually shrieked when he saw it and then made some excuse to leave." Dom shrugged. "I think he's been struggling in class for a while now . . . finally figured out he can't just breeze through everything like he did in high school, so maybe he's finally cracked."

"Yeah, maybe," Drew said, hoping his *voice* didn't crack.

"But you're really okay?" Dom asked again, his voice full of concern. "I can just imagine how forceful he was." He shuddered.

Drew smiled at him, warm and genuine, lucky to have such a good friend. "Yeah, I am, I swear. Thanks, though. Can I get you anything? Coffee? Or a soda?"

"Coffee would be great, thanks."

Drew went over and switched on the electric kettle, still cradling Zach in his arms, and then paused. "Crap, it's only instant. Sorry, is that okay?"

Dom rolled his eyes. "Drew, it's *fine*. I drink instant at home as well, okay. Sure, I live in my parents' apartment, and they give me an allowance, but it's not massive. The odd coffee from the Starbucks on campus or the Timmy's on Fifth is the fanciest I get, okay?"

Drew blushed. "Okay, sorry."

Dom laughed. "If you don't stop this needless apologising, I'm going to smack you upside the head. Now stop it."

I knew there was a reason I liked him, Zach said, and he jumped out of Drew's arms and trotted over to Dom, meowing up at him.

"Oh, you want up?" Dom asked, and then leaned back in the chair to give Zach space to jump onto his lap. "Oh, that reminds me, I bought something for you."

"For me?" Drew asked, shocked.

Dom laughed again. "No, sorry, no gifts for you. I bought something for Noodle."

"Awww, that's so sweet of you," Drew exclaimed.

I do enjoy gifts, Zach agreed.

Dom searched in his bag and rummaged around until he pulled out a small colourful toy wrapped in plastic. "Do you have scissors?" he asked and took them when Drew handed over a pair.

If he expects me to play with a toy, *he is sadly mistaken,* Zach said haughtily.

I thought you liked gifts? Drew teased.

I thought it would be food!

Well, aren't you a fussy boots!

Dom finally got the plastic off, and Zach's head snapped up. *What is that smell?* he demanded. *It's divine, and that's coming from an angel!*

"What is it?" Drew asked as Dom held the toy out in front of Zach's face.

"It's a catnip toy," Dom explained. "Cats *love* them."

Zach's whole body was shaking and Drew could tell it was taking every inch of his willpower not to pounce on the toy. *Go on, give in, you know you want to.*

I. Am. Not. An. Animal. Zach gritted out, shaking so badly now his fluffy bottom was swinging from side to side.

I hate to break it to you, but at this very moment, you are, Drew told him.

I am above these base instincts! Zach continued to protest.

Dom frowned. "What's the matter, Noodle? You don't want it?" He shook the toy gently in front of Zach's face and it must have sent another whiff of the nip over to him.

Fuck, it smells so good! He all but wailed in Drew's mind, and then he pounced on the toy, batting it out of Dom's hand and then chasing it across the kitchen.

Drew and Dom got absolutely no studying done as they spent the following fifteen minutes watching a manic brown and white furball dart around the kitchen after the catnip. Zach no longer spoke in Drew's mind, either too embarrassed about being ruled by his feline form or too enthralled with the nip. He appeared to be having fun, though, so Drew didn't worry too much. Finally, he began to slow, and Dom stood up and crossed to him, picking him up and depositing him in Drew's arms. "Looks like it's finally wearing off. He'll just chill now, so we can get some work done."

They started studying, but Drew found he was too distracted to concentrate. Zach was flopped over in his lap, staring up at Drew and idly batting Drew's hoodie with his paw. Out loud he was making quiet, content meows and purrs, but in the silence of Drew's head, he was rambling on.

Have you ever, like, looked up at the stars and just marvelled at how shiny they are? Like, they're little balls of flame in the sky, but if you got close, they wouldn't be so little anymore, they'd be huge *and they'd burn you up, burn you up to a crisp, but don't you worry, Drew, my Drew, my sweetness, my love, the nasty star isn't going to burn you up because I'd fight it and I'd win, hands down, a stupid star has got* nothing *on me, because I love you so much and I'd protect you, keep you safe, because I love you. Did I mention that? I love you like so* much, *more than you'll ever know, more than you love those peppermint mochas. Who do you think came up with those? Who came up with mocha in the first place? Why would someone take coffee and decide to ruin it by adding chocolate to it? I think they were cowards, they clearly didn't like coffee because coffee was too badass for them so they took the coward's way out by adding chocolate and then some other maniac decided to go and add peppermint* to it. Like, who *does* that? I mean, *I would, but only because you like them and I love you. Did I mention that? You're like, the most perfect person to have ever personed and I'm so lucky that you suck at making chicken noodle soup, otherwise I'd never have met you. Fuck, I love you.*

Drew giggled and tried to cover it by coughing so Dom wouldn't think he was a complete moron for laughing at nothing. He sank the fingers of one hand into the soft fur of Zach's tummy and whispered silently in his mind, *I love you too.* With happiness overwhelming him, he pulled his textbook toward him and tried to concentrate.

Goats on Roof

It was a rare day off, and Drew and Zach had decided to get out of town for the day. Inspired by a daydream he'd had when things had first developed between them, Drew had wanted to head to Parksville to visit Todd and introduce him to Zach. Todd and his family were over on the mainland for the weekend, though, so he figured they could still head there and see the sand sculpting competition, then head over to the Old Country Market at Coombs. Kind of like a date. It made his stomach churn with nervous butterflies, even after their catnip-fuelled declarations, but Zach appeared as cool and calm as ever.

Zach had been willing to hire a car for the day, but Dom had graciously offered the use of his BMW in exchange for them bringing him back a few bags of the specialty coffee beans they sold at the market. Once they'd picked up the car, they stopped at Timmy's for cold brews, and then they were on the parkway heading north.

Turning his face towards the open window, Drew took a deep breath. The sun was warm on his skin, the wind was fresh, and he was feeling content. Happy. He felt a hand on his thigh and looked over to find Zach smiling gently at him. "Keep your eyes on the road," he admonished, even as he covered Zach's hand with his own.

"I'm not going to run us off the road," Zach assured him.

"Famous last words."

Zach snorted. "Sweetness, don't forget that I'm not human. I could drive with my eyes closed and we'd be fine."

"Yeah, but we'd end up getting pulled over by every traffic cop who passed us," Drew pointed out. "That would kind of ruin our day."

"True," Zach conceded, and after a cheeky wink, turned his eyes back to the road in front of them.

They reached Parksville, and Drew directed Zach to the parking lot of the Parksville Community Park. It was early enough that there wasn't a massive crowd, so they found a park easily and then headed down towards the beach where a fenced-off area held the sandcastle competition. Drew was fast enough to buy their tickets before Zach could, having scrimped together a small amount of savings over the past couple of weeks so he was able to treat his angel every now and then without being one hundred percent reliant on his magic money card. He didn't have *much* pride left, but the bit that had survived needed these few moments, rare as they were.

Zach kissed his cheek in thanks and took his hand, and they strolled amongst the magnificent displays of sand and skill. There were monstrous sea creatures, fantastical beasts, and humans so expertly carved into the sand they could almost pass as portraits. They'd received tokens at the entrance, and they debated together over which sculptures to award their tokens to, thus casting their votes for the best piece. After circling around the area twice, Drew awarded his token to a scene of dogs playing poker, and Zach to the kraken attacking a sailing ship.

They left the sculptures behind and made their way down to the beach itself. The tide was out, revealing a vast stretch of grey sand beyond the rocks. Large logs littered the shoreline, and they picked their way carefully around them to walk out towards the ocean.

There were few people around, so Drew took the time to find his centre. He felt the magic within him build, and after one last furtive look around for witnesses, directed it towards the sand at his feet and whispered, *"fiat pulcher"* Millions of grains of sand rose into the air, whirling and circling as he directed them. Using his hands as a guide, he took the picture in his mind and transformed the sand to its likeness. Once done, a miniature version of Zach—complete with wings—rose from the beach.

He eyed it critically and then turned to Zach. "It's not perfect, but I think with some prac—oomph." His words were cut off by Zach's mouth on his. Strong arms wrapped around his waist and pulled him close, even as Zach's tongue plunged into his mouth. When Zach finally broke the kiss, Drew gazed up at him, slightly dazed. "What was that for?"

"You are a gift, Drew," Zach told him, his whiskey-coloured eyes sparkling in the morning sun. "I've rarely met anyone with a heart as pure as yours."

He could feel himself getting bashful. "It's just a sand sculpture," he said. "And I cheated by using magic to make it."

"That doesn't make it any less precious to me," Zach said, his words laced with sincerity.

Not knowing how to respond to that, Drew just gave him a shy smile, and turned to keep walking. Of course, it was at that precise moment his feet got tangled and he fell over, completely crushing the sculpture as he face planted.

"Well, it was nice while it lasted," Zach drawled, even as he helped him to his feet and brushed off the sand.

They pulled into a parking spot in front of the Old Country Market in Coombs, and Zach gazed up at the building in front of them, a furrow between his brow. "Huh," he said.

Drew grinned. "Not what you were expecting?"

"Have you slipped me some 'nip or am I actually seeing a goat on the roof?"

"It's what the market is famous for," Drew told him. He opened the car door and got out, taking the time to scan the grassed area on top of the market. He could see one goat munching away on the grass above where he knew the restaurant to be, but he couldn't see the other goat anywhere. He was pretty sure there were only two at the moment, but in the past there had been more.

"I guess as gimmicks go," Zach said as he joined him. "It's not half bad."

Drew made them grab a selfie with the goat behind them, and then dragged Zach across the small street, away from the market. "Come on, let's get an ice cream and explore the other stores first, and then we can check out the market."

They got large scoops of ice cream—strawberry cheesecake for Drew, and tiger tail for Zach—and then they made their way slowly around the handful of stores that surrounded a large square which was filled with a random assortment of stone statues. Inside the Coombs Emporium, that sold a mix of clothing and household items, they came across an intricately carved chair in the shape of a penis. Zach waggled his eyebrows suggestively at Drew, who licked his ice cream lasciviously in response, before they broke into childish giggles. A stern look from the woman at the cash register made them laugh even harder, and they scurried from the store before she could kick them out.

They bought squares of fudge from a sweet shop, and Zach found a ratty old copy of *The Complete Sherlock Holmes Collection* at the secondhand book store. "One of the demons brought this back with him after a summoning in the 1930s," he explained as he tucked it into a tote shopping bag after purchasing it. "I couldn't even tell you how many times I read it. It was definitely my favourite."

Once they'd looked into the crumbling castle that sat sentry on the roadside, they made their way over to the market proper. Drew had always loved the old market. It was packed to the brim with a vast array of goods, from groceries, toys, homewares, international foods, and even a suit of armour. Colourful lanterns hung from the ceiling, and everywhere they turned, the yellow and black Goats on Roof logo was there, plastered across T-shirts, bumper stickers, labels, and more.

They browsed the aisles for over an hour, playing with the wooden toys, stocking up on Billy Gruff blend coffee beans for Dom, and selecting some heat-n-eat savoury pastries from the display cabinet to take home for dinner.

"Are you sure we couldn't just make them ourselves?" Drew asked, wincing a little at how much they cost. "We could stop at a Country Grocer on the way home and pick up some ingredients."

"Sweetness, I love you, but no," Zach told him solemnly as he guided him away from the counter.

"It can't be that hard to do," Drew grumbled. "Surely I couldn't muck it up *that* badly."

"Two words. Beelzebub and Asmodeus," Zach said, not unkindly.

Drew's shoulders slumped in defeat. "Okay, fine. Point taken. I was just trying to save us some money."

"And once again I'll remind you that you don't have to do that. A couple of sausage rolls isn't going to break the bank." Zach turned Drew and began to march him towards the rear of the market where the cafe was. "Speaking of food, I'm hungry, so let's get some lunch."

They were just passing the suit of armour when it happened. Drew watched the events unfold almost in slow motion, as two boys ran full pelt around the corner, chasing one another. The first boy, too busy looking over his shoulder to watch where he was going, collided with the armour with an almighty crash. The armour swayed on the spot and very slowly began to topple over, directly towards an elderly woman who was looking at little boxes in the shape of books.

Drew didn't even think, he simply reacted. Without consciously finding his centre, he drew upon his magic and directed it towards the armour. The only Latin word he could think of in the moment was "*stet,*" but it was enough to do the trick. Mid-fall, the armour reversed direction until it was back upright, rocking slightly but in no danger of flattening someone's grandma.

The people nearby who had witnessed the near miss all began to talk about how lucky the woman had been, even as the parents of the boys began to scold them for running in the store. No one appeared to have noticed anything out of the ordinary, putting it down to luck.

Avoiding the small crowd, Zach manoeuvred them towards the cafe and found them a seat. Drew sank down into a chair, placing his hands flat against the roughly hewn wood of the table, needing it to ground him. "Shit," he whispered, squeezing his eyes shut. "I almost gave away the fact I can do magic."

"But you didn't," Zack assured him, as he sat in the chair next to him. "Instead, you saved that woman from being injured."

"But what if—"

"Drew," Zack said firmly, cutting him off. "Don't go down the 'what if' path. Just focus on the positives. You prevented harm from befalling someone, *and* you demonstrated that using your powers is becoming more instinctual." He wrapped an arm around Drew's shoulders and pressed a kiss to his cheek. "You did good, sweetness."

"Yeah?" Drew asked, needing the validation.

"Yeah," Zach agreed. "Now, let's get some lunch and head home. I think the perfect way to end this date will be to curl up in bed together and watch a movie."

Beaming at his angel, Drew could only agree. "I like the way you think.

Showdown

Drew hurried across campus, running late for his morning class after Zach had delayed him with a blow job that morning. The past couple of weeks had been non-stop for him, between uni assignments ramping up and Kensington demanding more and more of his time for training. He'd finally mastered the basics of wielding his power and had moved on to more advanced magic. It was absolutely exhausting and there was very little time left over for any bedroom shenanigans. He'd absolutely not been complaining when Zach had pushed him against the back of the door and dropped to his knees after breakfast, but it was a little inconvenient now he was so late.

Zach's voice thundered in his head commanding him to *STOP!* and he staggered to a halt.

"What is it? What's wrong?" Drew asked out loud, his head twisting from side to side to try and see where the danger was.

Something's wrong, Zach said, wriggling his cat form out of Drew's backpack and climbing onto his shoulder. *Can you not feel that?*

Drew concentrated, tuning out the noise and commotion of the busy university campus. Then he felt it, the change in pressure of the atmosphere surrounding them, but it was coming from all around him, not just one direction, which is why he hadn't noticed it. "Magic? But who? Why?"

"Drew!" he heard being called out from behind him, and he turned to see Gwen and Dom crossing the quad, waving at him. In their wake trailed a sullen Edward, clearly annoyed that the others were trying to act like he wasn't there.

He didn't bother returning the greeting, too busy trying to figure out where the magic users were and what they were doing.

"Is something wrong?" Dom asked as he noticed Drew's expression.

Drew nodded but didn't—couldn't—explain, his eyes continuing to dart around.

It's all around us. Should I call Kensington? he asked silently.

It wouldn't hurt, Zach agreed.

Sending a quick text off to the sorcerer, not really wanting to explain out loud while other people were around, Drew pocketed his phone and tried once more to narrow down where the magic was coming from, but it was too noisy, too busy. There were just too many distractions.

"What the hell is wrong?" Gwen asked, picking up on the vibe. "You look like you've seen a ghost."

From one side, there came a loud noise, and they all turned to see what it was. The concrete under a seating area was cracking, breaking apart as the ground beneath it began to lift.

From the opposite direction came the sounds of screams, and when Drew whipped his head around, he saw the lawn was erupting, chunks of dirt and turf flying high into the air. It was then that he caught a glimpse of someone nearby, a book open in their palms, and they appeared to be chanting.

"Oh, fuck," he whispered.

Oberon. Zach said the name as if it were a curse and then he was leaping from Drew's shoulder, transforming into his normal form, his eyes blazing.

"Werecat!" Edward squealed, pointing at Zach, eyes wide.

Everyone ignored him, too busy being horrified as the ground around them continued to churn and break apart. Then there were more screams as hands appeared, clawing their way up and out of the ground. The bodies of the demons followed, some of them human-looking the way Beelzebub and Asmodeus had been, others with deformed bodies and hellish features. Panic broke out as students began to run for their lives.

"Go, get out of here!" Drew told his friends. "Run!"

Dom grabbed Gwen's hand and they started to run away, but then stopped as the earth in front of them broke open and something else began to emerge. Gwen screamed and they turned, but by now they were blocked in, with no escape.

Two beams of bright light shot through the air and Drew breathed a sigh of relief as Kensington and Simon appeared next to them. The Grand Master took in the situation with a single glance and looked over at Zach. "Friends of yours, I assume?"

"They are no friends of mine," Zach snarled.

Drew grabbed Dom's arm and tugged him and Gwen behind him then, feeling generous, he also grabbed Edward and pushed him back as well. "Stay behind me," he instructed.

"What the hell is going on?" Dom asked, his voice shaky.

"Long story short . . . Zach is an angel who was trapped in hell by an asshole fallen angel, and it looks like he's come for him."

"Ah, right, okay." Dom looked around. "Not the answer I expected, but given the evidence before me it kinda makes sense."

"If they want Zach, just give him to them!" Edward cried, eyeing the approaching horde of demons with fear. "There's no need for us to get caught in the middle!"

"You keep up talk like that and I'll throw you to them myself," Kensington growled at Edward, and then with a sharp gesture at Simon and Zach, they joined Drew and formed a circle around the three students, facing outwards towards the threat. "Zach, what's the best way to deal with these guys?"

"Other than pray?" Zach shook his head. "They're powerful, but they can be killed. Brute force will do it."

"Okay, then, brute force it is." And with that, Kensington sent a wave of magic through the air at the demons approaching from his side. The magic hit them with a concussive force, sending them flying backward, ripping through their bodies as it went. The demons howled, but of the five who were caught up in the blast, only two got back to their feet.

Drew reached out and caught Zach's hand, squeezing it tightly. "I won't let him take you back," he promised.

Zach gave him a small smile and said, "Be safe." Then he let go and charged at the oncoming demons.

Drew reached deep within himself, finding the spark of power he knew resided there. He felt it curling together, building in strength, ready to be released, and he didn't bother with grace or finesse, didn't use any of the phrases that Kensington had taught him to channel the energy, he just let it loose. With a cry, he flung a ball of pure magic outwards, and it flew forward, incinerating the three demons who were in its direct path. With a hand outstretched, he hooked his hand, directing the magic to veer to the right, aiming for another demon. It cut through its chest with as much deadly force as it had taken down the others, and so he curled his hand again and sent it curving around to take out another fiend. By the time it ran out of enough force to inflict killing blows, eleven demons had been felled, but for each one that died, another three rose up to take its place, clawing at the earth and charging into the fray.

"Simon!" Kensington called. "We need to take out those who are summoning them, otherwise they'll just keep coming."

"On it," Simon said, opening what appeared to be a portal in front of two demons and shoving them through it, only to close it before they were all the way through, severing their bodies in half.

Drew saw Simon move out of his periphery, but he couldn't spare the attention to see if he was successful in dealing with the magic users, too engrossed in taking out as many of the demons as he could. He still couldn't see anyone who appeared to be in charge of them, and so he assumed that Oberon hadn't revealed himself yet, waiting until the tide turned in his favour.

He soon found himself fighting side by side with Zach, and they moved almost as one, calling warnings to each other silently in their minds, synchronising their movements to inflict the most amount of damage on the most amount of demons. It was like a dance—or their lovemaking—graceful and harmonised, the two of them moving about each other fluidly.

Above them, black clouds had begun to form, churning in the sky. The scent of ozone was heavy in the air and lightning flickered and danced across the clouds. The sheer amount of magic being flung around was creating a magically-charged storm, but Drew couldn't spare any energy to worry about the damage it might do. They needed to deal with the immediate threat of the demons and other magic users first. Then they could deal with the storm.

There was a bright flash of light from off to the side and Drew shielded his eyes. When he was able to see again, three winged figures stood in the quad, almost glowing as if lit from within with a heavenly light.

"Daniel?" Zach gasped, his eyes wide as he gaped at the newcomers.

A tall dark-skinned angel with pale green wings grinned. "Hey, Zachariel. Good to see you, brother."

"What are you doing here?"

"Hashmal, Adriel, and I thought you could use a hand," Daniel replied, gesturing to the others.

"You know, since we couldn't help last time," the angel who Drew assumed was Hashmal said. He was tall and graceful, with kind eyes that glowed almost as white as his wings.

"We tried, Zach, we did," Adriel said, her words oozing sincerity. Dark blue wings flared in contrast to her white-blonde hair. "We're here to make up for that."

Zach threw his head back and laughed. "Oh, I am *so* glad to see you guys."

Daniel grinned and then tilted his head at the battle. "Come on then. Let's get to it."

The three angels jumped into the fight and immediately the pressure was lessened, the tide turning. The wave of demons seemed to dwindle just a little, and Drew and Zach fought easier, still side by side.

Then a demon managed to break through their defences and it lunged for Dom, Gwen, and Edward. Dom shoved the others behind him and raised his arms, a feeble attempt to stop the attack. He cried out as a long claw sliced through his forearms but he didn't back down. He kept his body shielding the others, even as blood dripped down his arms.

"Don't even *think* about touching my friend," Zach snapped, approaching the demon from behind and grabbing it around the throat. With one brutal twist, he removed the demon's head from its shoulders and tossed it aside. "You good?" he asked Dom, wiping a spray of blood from his cheek with the back of his hand.

Dom nodded, panting in pain. "Yeah, thanks."

Gwen appeared at Dom's side, her eyes full of worry as she clamped a hand over the wound. Wisps of her hair were standing on end, charged by the storm. "What the hell is going on with the weather?" she asked, needing to raise her voice to almost a shout as the wind began to howl around them.

"It's a side effect of so much magic," Zach explained.

"Is it dangerous?" Dom said, his face still taut with pain.

Before Zach could even reply, a bolt of lightning struck the ground only metres from them. They all cried out and Drew found himself on the ground, Zach shielding his body with his own.

Edward shrieked and rolled himself into a ball, covering his head with his hands.

"Well, fuck me," Dom said from his position crouched on the ground, Gwen tucked under him. "I suppose that answers that question."

"We're getting on top of the demons," Drew told them. "If you see a gap and you think you've got a chance to make it, run. Okay?"

"But what about you?" Gwen demanded.

"I'll be fine," Drew assured her, even as he threw another wave of concussive magic at a group of approaching demons. "Zach's got my back. Promise me you'll make a run for it if you can."

Dom nodded. "We will. I'll make sure of it."

"Good man," Zach said and smiled at them. He turned back towards Drew, his mouth open to say something but it was cut off by a scream. He clutched at his chest and fell to his knees on the broken concrete.

"Zach!" Drew cried, sending another blast of magic at the closest demons before darting over to the angel. "Zach, what's wrong? What is it?"

Zach couldn't reply, the pain too great, but then Drew saw it, the purple gem in his chest pulsating with energy through the material of his shirt. "Drew," Zach finally managed to utter, his eyes locked on a point over Drew's shoulder. "Go, it's too late. He's h . . . here."

Drew looked behind him and saw a tall bald man with flashing silver eyes striding through the demons as if he were taking an afternoon stroll in the park. An old-fashioned cane with a gold tip swung from his right hand. His sharp gaze fell on Zach and he grinned, then he lifted his finger and made a hooking gesture, and Zach cried out again even as he was yanked to his feet by an invisible force. Lightning crashed above them, immediately followed by the deafening roar of the thunder. "My, my, Zachariel, what an interesting adventure you've been having," the man, who Drew assumed was Oberon, said.

"Jealous?" Zach asked, managing a sneer, before he screamed once more as whatever Oberon was doing to the gem intensified.

"Oh, no, not at all. In fact, I've enjoyed watching your antics. It's been a little like reality TV." His eyes flicked over to Drew. "You even have a love interest." He shook his head and tsked. "Zachariel, Zachariel, Zachariel. Whatever convinced you that I would allow you to be *happy?* Your fate is in my hands, and that will only ever involve suffering."

"I beg to differ," Zach ground out through the pain.

Oberon snorted. "Always so stubborn." He hooked his finger again, and Zach screamed, clawing at the gem, trying to remove it from his chest. His nails tore through his shirt and then at his flesh. Blood ran in dark rivulets down his skin, soaking into the material and turning it crimson.

"Stop it!" Drew screamed, hurling a ball of magic at Oberon.

The demon laughed and flicked the magic away as if it were nothing more irritating than a mosquito. "Oh, you are precious. I'm going to have fun making you suffer." His grin faded as a force hit him from behind and Drew looked over to see Kensington there, throwing ropes of golden magic at him.

"You'll have to go through me first," Kensington challenged, and Simon must have disabled the magic users who'd been summoning the demons because Drew noticed that less than twenty demons were remaining. Simon, Daniel, Hashmal, and Adriel were easily taking care of them.

Oberon roared and lunged into a fight with Kensington, and Drew turned his attention to Zach. The clouds above them opened and a torrent of rain began to fall, soaking them instantly. He lowered Zach to the ground and ripped away the torn remnants of his shirt, revealing the brightly glowing gem in his chest. The pulsating purple light had a sickly sheen to it that made Drew's stomach clench just from looking at it. "Zach, can you hear me?" he asked, stroking his cheek.

"Hey, sweetness," Zach whispered, his eyes fluttering open as he looked up at him. His lashes were thick with droplets of rain and he blinked them away. "We had a good run, didn't we? I'm sorry it couldn't last."

"Oh, don't you dare take that defeatist attitude with me," Drew growled. "You're not going anywhere."

"So long as he controls the gem, I cannot be free," Zach whispered.

"Then we'll just have to do something about that, won't we?" Drew dropped his hand down from Zach's face, trailing over his collarbones until it was hovering over the gem. "Do you trust me?"

"With everything I have," Zach said.

Drew smiled and leaned down to kiss him gently. "I love you, Zach."

"And I love you.""And love will set you free," Drew whispered, then closed his eyes and concentrated.

The magic of the gem was stronger than anything Drew had ever felt before, nothing at all like the objects he had studied with Kensington. No matter how strong it was, Drew knew he was stronger. He'd been told that by Zach and Kensington, and deep down inside himself, he could feel his strength and he believed it too. Ignoring the storm and the rain, the ongoing battle and screams of pain, he found his centre. He felt the magic jump to do his bidding and it poured from him. He directed it towards the gem and it twisted around it, tendrils of magic searching and seeking, looking for cracks in its power. The power of the gem seemed to be almost sentient, and it fought back, each surge of power blocking Drew's magic and making Zach convulse and cry out.

"You will never hurt my love again," Drew gritted out and forced all of his power, all the love he felt for his angel into the gem, overwhelming it, filling it up until it was brimming with magic. His own power worked to smother, to block the magic of the gem from entering Zach's body, stopping the pain, soothing the sting, a magical kiss to make it better. Zach slumped in relief as the pain ceased, and his eyes fell closed. Drew turned his attention deeper into the centre of the gem, finding the source of its power—the spell Oberon had used to create the gem in the first place. It was strong, but Drew was stronger, and he concentrated with all of his might, sending everything he had to the core, willing it to break. The gem absorbed the magic Drew channelled into it and so he reached even deeper within himself and fed it even more. He could tell it was reaching its limit, he just had to keep going. He was beginning to flag, his reserves used up, but he pushed himself just a little more.

This was for Zach. He would do this for Zach.

Feeling completely drained but digging even deeper, he found one last reserve of power and pushed it into the gem. A sound like a bell rang out, and the glow of the gem began to fade. Once the light had dimmed completely, it cracked in half and fell from Zach's chest, leaving the indent of a scar in its place.

Zach heaved in a deep breath and his eyes snapped open. He sat up and threw himself into Drew's arms, and Drew cradled him close, providing him with a measure of privacy as he processed the fact his shackles had finally been broken.

From across the quad came a scream of anger, and Drew looked over to see Oberon glaring at him with hate in his eyes. "You took him from me!" he raged, and then he threw Kensington to one side and lunged towards Drew.

Drew had absolutely nothing left. He reached for his magic but his well of power had run dry. He hunched over Zach, knowing his feeble human body would provide little protection, but it was the only thing he had left.

Then the three angels were there, landing in front of him, their wings flaring. Oberon came to a halt as his path was blocked.

"It's over," Daniel told him. "Your hold on Zachariel is broken. You *will* return to the depths of Hell from whence you came."

"You have no power over me, angel," Oberon spat, and he raised his arms to blast them with a spell.

A tiny flicker of light left his hands and fizzled out in the pouring rain.

"What the fuck?" Oberon growled, staring at his hands like he'd never seen them before. It appeared his words were simply that—words. Whatever power he'd had seemed to have diminished with the destruction of the gem.

"Move in," Daniel barked and the three angels rushed in, easily overpowering Oberon. He screamed and cursed, fighting for all his worth, but he was no match for the angels. Daniel tackled him to the ground, and Hashmal pulled out a simple-looking rope and used it to bind his wrists. It must have been magically enhanced because no matter how fiercely Oberon fought its bonds as Adriel pulled him to his feet, the rope did not loosen.

"Give it up," Adriel snapped at him, shoving him forward until Oberon walked towards the others. Her pale hair was plastered to her face from the rain but she still managed to look regal and powerful as she guarded her prisoner.

Daniel turned to Zach and held out a hand. Zach clasped it warmly, pulling the other angel into a hug. "Thank you," he said, his voice hoarse from his screams of pain.

"It's the least we could do," Daniel told him. He then paused as the hug finished and he grasped Zach by both shoulders. "You can come home, Zachariel, now you're free." He smiled. "Come with us?"

Zach smiled but shook his head. "The years down below have changed me, Daniel. I'm not an angel anymore."

"We disagree. You may have scars, but you're still worthy of your wings."

Drew could see that Zach was tempted but let out a sigh of relief when he stepped away from Daniel and twined his fingers with Drew's. "Thank you, but my place is here."

"You're sure?" Daniel asked.

"Let it be, Daniel," Hashmal said. "It's clear to anyone that he's in love with the human. Let him have his happy ending—he deserves it."

Zach beamed at Hashmal and then winked. "And a happy one it will be."

Hashmal laughed and then tilted his head at Daniel. "Come on, let's get going. We have this piece of trash to drop off down below before we go home, and it's a long journey to the borderlands."

Daniel clapped Zach on the back one last time. "Be good, man."

"I make no promises," Zach teased. "I'm living with humans now and they're all about the grey."

Daniel laughed and then Drew blinked and the three angels and their prisoner were gone.

Silence fell over the quad—except for the rain that was starting to ease—as everyone caught their breaths. The clouds above were still dark, but slightly less black than they'd been earlier, the magic in them slowly dissipating.

Drew wrapped his arm around Zach's waist and supported them both as they stood together, processing the events that had just unfolded.

It was over. They'd won and Zach was free.

"What the fuck just happened?" Edward demanded, shoving his way towards them.

Drew shook his head and chuckled. "Something much bigger than were-animals," he said.

"Edward, give me your shirt," Gwen demanded before Edward could press for more answers. "I need something to bandage Dom's arms with."

Edward glared at her. "Why does it have to be *mine*? This is a Hermès shirt. Do you know how much this cost? It's too good to be used as a rag. Why can't you use Drew's instead?"

Zach leaned towards him and growled. "You're not getting to see Drew half naked in any lifetime, so give her your damn shirt."

Edward jumped back in fright, ripping off his dripping shirt and flinging it at Gwen. As she tore it into long strips and began to wrap Dom's arms, Kensington and Simon approached. "That was a nice piece of magic," Kensington complimented Drew.

"Thanks," he said with a blush.

"Why don't you and Zach head home," he offered. "Simon and I will take care of the cleanup here. Go and have a well-earned break. You deserve it."

"Are you sure? Isn't explaining all this going to be an absolute clusterfuck?" He gestured around at the destruction and the groups of terrified students who were beginning to emerge from their hiding spots.

Kensington smiled. "I'm positive. This sort of thing actually falls under my job description. Take the rest of the day, but if you're free tomorrow, come to the Collective. I've found something that might interest you."

Drew nodded. "Okay. I'm not going to argue with you since I'm dead on my feet. We'll come see you tomorrow." He looked over at Dom and Gwen. "You'll take care of my friends?"

"I will," Kensington promised.

Drew managed a smile. "Thanks. Edward, though . . . do what you want with him. I don't particularly care."

Kensington chuckled. "Oh, we'll be having a little debrief, and let's just say we might stray into other areas during that conversation."

"What?" Edward squawked. "What are you going to do to me? I'm a victim here! You can't treat me like this. I have rights!"

Ignoring Edward, they waved at Dom and Gwen, then Zach took his hand and they began to walk away, steps heavy with exhaustion. "Bed sounds good right now," Drew said with a yawn.

"Yes it does," Zach said. "Let's get back to your place as quickly as we can."

"I think you mean *our* place," Drew corrected him.

Zach paused, then leaned over to kiss Drew on the cheek. "Let's go *home.*"

And as they walked, Drew felt the heavy weight of a wing fall across his shoulders.

A New Start

Z ach snaked a feather-light touch down Drew's spine with a wingtip, leaving goosebumps in its wake. Drew shivered and dipped his head to capture Zach's lips in another kiss, his tongue brushing lightly over Zach's. "Feels so good," he murmured.

They had stumbled home and into the shower before falling into bed, utterly exhausted, and had napped for a solid five hours, both needing the rest. But they were both wide awake now.

Zach smiled up at him. "I like making you feel good, Drew. Just wait until I show you how else I can use them."

Drew cocked a brow. "Really?" he asked, sounding half sceptical, half curious.

Zach's smile morphed into a wolfish grin and he flipped them so Drew was on his back, spread out below him. "Oh, sweetness, you have *no* idea." He leaned back, giving himself room to work, and then trailed both his wings from Drew's feet all the way up over his body, being sure to brush against his heavily leaking cock as he passed it by. Drew gasped and Zach drank it in, loving every whimper and moan that he wrung out of his lover.

He couldn't believe Drew had actually managed to free him, that he'd broken the chains the gem had him locked in. The weight of the wings on his back was comforting, though his shoulders burned a little from using muscles he hadn't exercised in years. It would take time to rebuild his strength before he could fly, but he could picture it now . . . soaring above the city, Drew in his arms, showing him what the world looked like from above. There would be time for that later. They had the rest of their lives together now, and so there was no rush. No, for now he would take his time, lay claim to Drew and have their own private celebration of the battle they'd won that morning.

His feathers brushed over Drew's cheek, caressing the deep scratch that marred his skin, a souvenir of the fight. It was the only injury Drew had sustained, a testament to his strength and power, of how easily he had destroyed all in his path. Zach had once thought he knew what real power was, but everything he'd ever experienced was nothing in comparison to the magic Drew could wield. It didn't frighten him, though, he wasn't wary or worried. Drew had shown how far he would go to protect Zach, and Zach knew Drew would never use his power against him. This was the first time in his very long life he'd been with someone stronger than himself, but it didn't bother him. It made him feel safe and cherished.

And yet, Drew was still innocent in so many ways. Zach could still teach him, guide him, and explore everything they wanted to do together. This was just one of those things.

He dragged his right wing back down Drew's body, and then flexed and curled the feather around Drew's cock, forming a warm, tight, silky channel. Drew gasped and his hips bucked as Zach stroked him, watching Drew's face closely to make sure he was on board.

"Fuck, Zach," Drew swore, his eyes rolling back in his head.

"You like this? Does it feel good, sweetness?"

"God, don't stop. Please don't stop."

Zach had no intention of stopping and he continued to stroke Drew's cock, his feathers skimming easily across the velvety soft skin. His own cock twitched and dribbled against his thigh, but he ignored it, too engrossed in the blissful expression on Drew's face and the sounds he was making.

"Harder, please," Drew begged, arching upwards, thrusting his cock deep into Zach's wing.

Zach tightened his grip, flexing several times until he had the pressure right, and he felt Drew's cock throb in return. "You look so beautiful like this," he whispered, brushing another kiss across Drew's mouth. "So beautiful."

"Oh, fuck, Zach, I'm gonna come!" Drew cried, and then he was shuddering and Zach felt warm fluid coat his feathers.

"That's it, sweetness, yeah, so good for me, just like that," he crooned, working Drew through his orgasm.

Drew lay panting on the bed as Zach got up to fetch a washcloth to wipe himself off. The only problem with what they'd just done was cooling semen soon became glue-like and he'd lose a few feathers if he didn't clean up now. Sadly, that was a lesson he had learned the hard way.

Once he was done, he returned to the bed, and Drew pulled him down, his hand going immediately to Zach's cock, finding it still hard as a rock. "Can I suck you?" Drew asked, looking up at Zach from under his lashes.

Zach snorted. "As if you even need to ask. Of course you can."

Drew smiled, then licked his lips, and that action alone made Zach almost come right there and then. The things that Drew *did* to him!

Drew moved down the bed and licked a stripe up Zach's cock, then twirled his tongue around the crown. Once he'd gotten the tip nice and wet, he slid his mouth down over the shaft, taking in as much as he could, his hand working the bottom few inches. Zach sighed at how good it felt and reached down to sink his fingers into Drew's soft locks, fisting the hair near the scalp and tugging gently. Drew groaned and rubbed himself against Zach's calf, his cock growing hard once more.

The adrenaline still pumping through Zach's veins from the confrontation with Oberon had Zach's heart beating hard, and he found himself on edge far quicker than he liked. He grasped Drew's hair more firmly, slowing him down, and thrust shallowly into his mouth. "So good, sweetness. Fuck, you should see what this looks like."

Drew tried to look up at him but the angle made it hard. Zach tilted Drew's head back so he could meet his gaze, and his cock slipped almost all the way out of Drew's mouth. Tonguing around the head, Drew kept his eyes locked on Zach's, who reached out and swiped away a bead of saliva that was running down Drew's chin. Pulling off completely, Drew said in a hoarse voice, "I love you." Then he leaned down and took Zach as deep as he could, working the last few inches with his hand.

Now that Drew was on a mission to make him come, Zach didn't last much longer, and as soon as he reached the edge, he pulled free of Drew's mouth and spurted all over his chest. Once he'd finished shuddering through his orgasm, he grabbed his shirt from the floor and wiped his cum off Drew's skin, then he flopped back down on the bed, breathing hard. Drew snuggled up next to him, his head on Zach's chest and his erection pressing against Zach's thigh. "Do you want me to take care of that?" he asked.

He felt Drew shake his head. "I'm good. Happy just to cuddle."

Zach smiled and bent down to press a kiss to Drew's hair, then wrapped both wings around him and held him close. Even breathing soon told him that Drew had fallen asleep again, despite the long nap they'd already had. Given the power he'd expended that day, Zach wouldn't be surprised if he didn't surface again until morning.

Even though he was also tired again, Zach didn't allow sleep to take him for some hours. He gazed in wonder down at the human in his arms, and let his imagination run wild with all the things the future had in store for him with Drew by his side.

It wasn't long after they knocked at the door to the Nightingale Collective that Simon answered, welcoming both Drew and Zach inside. He raised a brow at Zach who raised one higher in reply. "What?" he asked after their standoff had been going on so long that Drew started laughing. He still found the eyebrow thing rather ridiculous, but there was no way he was going to tell them that.

"You're a little conspicuous, don't you think?" Simon asked.

Zach flexed his wings and Drew did his best not to swoon right there and then. Zach's wings *did* things to him, and after last night's experience he was sure he was blushing.

"Oh, you mean these?" Zach asked with faux innocence.

Simon rolled his eyes. "Yes, those, with the eight-foot wingspan!"

Zach flapped them several times, sending a brisk wind blowing through the entrance hall. "Don't worry, no one but other magic users can see them, and then only if I want them to."

"I'm more concerned about you breaking something delicate and irreplaceable," came a stern voice from behind Simon, and Drew turned to see Kensington glaring at Zach whilst pushing a delicate-looking chalice further back on its display table. "Put them away, Zach!"

Zach pouted again, and Drew laughed out loud as he made a show of folding his wings back.

Kensington rolled his eyes at Zach's antics and then welcomed them inside. "Come on back. Can I get anyone some tea?"

Drew accepted, while Zach requested coffee instead, and Kensington being the gentleman that he was, willed some into existence. "How are you holding up after yesterday?" Kensington asked Drew.

"Okay, I guess. I'm still a little tired but doing okay."

"That's to be expected from the amount of power you expended. Make sure you rest up over the next few days and try to keep your magic use to a minimum."

"Were there any . . . complications, from the cleanup?" Drew asked, worried about the fallout. He'd sent Dom and Gwen messages but their replies about their debriefings had been short and vague. Their messages asking to see him soon so they could get the whole story from him were much longer and demanding.

"No, we managed to get everything sorted, don't fret about that," Kensington assured him.

Drew wondered how they could possibly have explained away everything to the police, not to mention the hundreds of students who had been witnesses, but he brushed aside his concerns for now. Kensington would surely have his ways, and Drew was much more curious about the reason he'd been invited around in the first place. "So, you wanted to show me something?"

"Ah, yes." He clicked his fingers and a scroll flew across the room into his grasp. He unrolled it and placed it on the table, weighing down the corners with his teacup, the sugar bowl, the milk jug, and a spare book. "I was doing some research into your family tree and I believe I've found the reason for your powers."

"You have?" Drew asked, dumbfounded.

"Yes. Have you ever looked into your history before?"

Drew shook his head. "Not really. Aunt Harriett tried to get hold of a family tree for me when I was a kid, just after my parents died, but she couldn't really find anything about my mom's side of the family and it only went back a couple of generations on my father's side. There doesn't seem to be anything before my great-grandparents."

"Well, that would be because your family went underground for several centuries," Kensington told him. "It started back in England in the late fifteen hundreds when one of your relatives was burned at the stake for practising witchcraft. Of course, little did the authorities know, but she wasn't all that powerful. Her *mother,* on the other hand, was and she was *pissed.* Magdalene Fitzpatrick was hell-bent on revenge and she didn't just kill those who murdered her daughter, she made them suffer. Then, once she had finished with them, she went on a crusade of sorts, hunting down witch finders and stopping them before they could kill any more witches. It was during this that she met Gerald Reilly, a powerful warlock, and they fell in love. Gerald had also lost loved ones to the persecution of magic users and he was more than eager to help Magdalene with her quest."

"Holy shit," Drew said, half in awe and half in horror.

"They soon became an unstoppable force," Kensington continued. "But of course, that just made them a target. A group of hunters got together to find them and burn them, and in doing so, began to murder those closest to the pair, even if they showed no magical inclination whatsoever. In the end, to keep their families safe, the pair faked their deaths and went into hiding. They formed an underground magic movement and became teachers so others could learn from them. Their children showed great aptitude for magic and their grandchildren even more so."

"And they managed to remain hidden?" Zach asked.

"Oh, yes. Quite successfully."

"That must have taken its toll on them," Drew said, a little sadly.

Kensington looked thoughtful. "We'll never really know, but from what I found, the pair were so dedicated to protecting their loved ones that I believe it would have been a sacrifice they were more than willing to make."

Drew shrugged and gave a sad smile. "Still, it can't have been easy."

"No, most likely not," Kensington agreed. "Not long after the proper death of Magdalene and Gerald, the family decided it was no longer safe for them in England, and they set sail for the States. There was some trouble during the late sixteen hundreds, but they remained hidden and avoided most of it. They continued teaching in secret, mentoring and guiding any magic users who sought out their help."

"They really dedicated their entire lives to teaching? My whole family?" Drew asked. His throat was a little tight from learning something so personal about the family he never even knew existed. Zach reached over and took his hand, holding it tightly.

"They did, while they could," Kensington explained. "Over time, the number of children born to your family with the ability dwindled, and so there were fewer people to pass on that knowledge. Those who were born with magic were incredibly powerful, almost as if the power was being distilled throughout the generations. It became harder and harder to find those who could teach, however, since their numbers were dwindling. There were several incidents of your relatives going their entire lives without ever knowing they had magic, not until something happened to set it off, usually causing their deaths." Kensington smiled. "Funnily enough, I found a record which stated that your great-great-great uncle was once part of our Collective, and was a close candidate to become the Grand Master. So you see, Drew, magic has been in your family for hundreds of years. We cannot be at all surprised by your strength."

Drew leaned back on the sofa, dumbstruck. His family was *full* of witches and warlocks and sorcerers and he'd never known. "Wow," he said, unable to find anything else to sum up the knowledge he'd just gained.

"Wow, indeed." Kensington sipped his tea. "Of course, this just reiterates the importance of continuing your training. Power such as yours cannot be untamed, lest you accidentally hurt someone. Up until now, I believe you have been training with the specific intent of helping Zachariel. I would like to officially extend my offer to help you master your abilities and help you discover your full potential."

Drew nodded. "Yes, please. That would be great."

Kensington nodded and then stood. "Well then, I won't keep you any longer today. You need your rest. I just wanted to share what I had found."

"Yeah, it was really interesting. Thank you."

"So, go home and rest up . . . and I'm serious about that. No magic for at least three days. After that, you may come around and we'll continue your lessons."

Drew followed Kensington to the door and Zach followed, one hand on Drew's lower back in a silent show of support. He held out a hand for Kensington to shake, and the sorcerer just snorted and pulled him into a hug. "Thank you," Drew whispered again.

"Anytime," Kensington said fondly. "Now, be off with you. I'm sure you and Zach have better things to be doing than having tea with me."

Zach waggled his brows, causing Drew to laugh and blush, then he gave Kensington a salute and guided Drew out the door and down onto the street. "So, sweetness, what shall we do with our day?"

"Hmmm." Drew gave it a moment's thought. "I know Dom and Gwen want some answers, so how about we have them over for dinner tonight so we can explain?"

"Sounds good. Do you think Dom would pet my tummy if I changed into my cat form?"

Drew snorted. "You're such a hussy, but I'm sure he will."

"Do you think he'll bring me some more nip?"

Laughing again, Drew said, "Maybe. If you ask nicely." Then he leaned over and kissed Zach on the cheek. "We'll need to stop by the shops on the way home and grab a few things."

"Uh, why?" Zach asked, suddenly wary.

"So I can cook dinner, of course. Duh!"

"Oh, Lord help us, this is *not* going to end well," Zach muttered.

But it did.

Epilogue

"Stop fidgeting," Drew chastised, putting his hand on Zach's knee in an effort to get it to stop bouncing.

They were on the bus heading to Victoria and were currently winding their way over the Malahat. Zach had been antsy the entire way and it was starting to drive Drew crazy.

"Sorry," Zach muttered and stilled his knee.

Drew started to count but he didn't even get to eighteen before the squirming began once more. "Honestly, what's got into you?" he asked. He couldn't fathom what would make someone as powerful as Zach so nervous.

"What if she doesn't like me?" Zach asked, chewing on his bottom lip.

Trying to be reassuring, Drew said, "She *already* likes you. You've spoken on the phone heaps of times. I think Harriett likes you better than she does me at this point."

"Only because she's not met me in person yet," Zach disagreed.

It was true they'd not had a chance to go and visit his aunt in the two months since the fight against Oberon. Between her shifts and Zach's assignments, their schedules hadn't aligned until now. Drew had told her about Zach, of course, and she'd demanded to speak to him on the phone. The one time they'd tried to have a FaceTime call, there had been "technical difficulties." Drew was well aware that Zach had used his magic to sabotage the call, but he'd not been able to wrangle an explanation from him as yet.

No time like the present.

"I thought you couldn't wait to meet Harriett? What's happened to make you so skittish?"

"I am not *skittish*!" Zach protested, giving Drew a petulant glare.

Drew just looked at him steadily—he'd been practising trying to raise just one eyebrow but the muscles in his face refused to cooperate and he just looked like he was having a stroke.

Even without the sophisticated eyebrow acrobatics, the look must have done something, because the fight went out of Zach in a rush and he sank down into his seat. "Urgh, *fine*. I might be a tad . . . nervous."

Drew frowned. "But why? She honestly thinks you're great."

Although they had plans to explain to Harriett about their family heritage and the magical world, they'd held off, as that was a conversation best had in person. Instead, they'd told her the story they'd originally given to Dom and Gwen—that they'd met when Zach moved into the apartment next door and Drew had helped him move some furniture.

"She made a comment," Zach said with a wince.

"What comment? About us?" No matter how hard he tried, Drew honestly couldn't see his aunt doing such a thing. She was very upfront, and if she had a problem with Zach, she would have told Drew outright.

"No, it wasn't about us, but it was *about us*," Zach said.

Huffing, Drew crossed his arms over his chest. "Gee, thanks. That's *really* cleared things up for me. I feel so informed right now."

Zach rolled his eyes. "No need to get snippy, sweetness."

"No need to be so fucking *vague*," Drew countered. "Just spit it out. What did Aunt Harriett say?"

"We'd been chatting about something . . . I honestly can't even remember what. Anyway, I made that stupid joke. You know the one—*still a better love story than Twilight*—and she started on this rant about what a terrible romance story that book was and how it was impossible to believe a man who was over a hundred years old could have anything in common with a teenager."

"Oh."

"Yes, oh. She made it very clear she thought Edward Cullen was a creepy old man who was taking advantage of a gormless teen girl simply because he stopped physically ageing at seventeen." Zach rolled his head over the headrest of the seat so he could look at Drew properly. "So yes, I'm nervous. Even before we tell her the truth about me, she'll probably already have an issue with me as I look like I'm twenty years older than you. When she finds out I'm actually closer to *two thousand* years older than you, I honestly think she'll kick me out on my ass."

Now it was Drew's turn to chew on his bottom lip as he thought about that. "Okay, so maybe we could just not tell her the truth?" Even to his own ears, it sounded false. There was no way in hell they were going to keep the truth from Harriett. That just wasn't the way their relationship worked. "Okay, so that's not gonna work. Look, maybe she *won't* have a problem with it? Maybe when faced with the situation in reality, she'll take a different viewpoint?"

"Do you really believe that?" Zach asked.

Drew sighed. "No."

There was a long silence and then Zach admitted in a quiet voice, "I'm worried she'll give you an ultimatum, and between me and her the choice is obvious. I'm scared I'm going to lose you."

Drew gripped Zach's hand tightly. "You will *not* lose me. We went through too much to be together, so don't even think that."

"Drew, we need to be realistic."

"Stop it," Drew commanded. "At the end of the day, I honestly believe Harriett just wants me to be happy. It might be a bit of a shock to her, but I love you. I'm not just going to give you up because she has some ethical issue with a sparkly assed vampire from a young-adult novel. She *likes* you, and I think the more she gets to know you, she'll like you even more. The age thing might be a bit of a shocker at first, but I honestly think it's not insurmountable."

Zach sighed but then raised their joined hands to his lips and pressed a kiss to Drew's knuckles. "I really hope you're right."

Throughout his long lifetime, Zach had fought demons, evil warlocks, and a number of other supernatural and magical creatures. He'd been cast into the deepest depths of Hell as an angel and had been tortured for countless months. He'd been in more hopeless situations than he cared to admit, and he'd lost count of the number of times he was sure the true death would take him.

None of that had ever scared him as much as the diminutive woman who sat in the armchair opposite him.

Harriett Phillips was five feet tall if she was an inch. She was slight in stature, with a strength which had surprised Zach when he'd watched her drag a heavy cabinet away from the wall after she'd dropped a bottle cap and it had rolled underneath it. She had the same pale blue eyes as Drew but her hair was lighter, closer to blonde. She was currently sitting with her feet tucked under her, a cup of coffee in one hand and an unreadable expression on her face.

Drew was currently levitating his own mug about two feet above the coffee table in a demonstration of his powers to go with the long and involved story they'd just told her. He slowly settled the mug down and then waved his hands about as if to say "Ta-da!."

Harriett didn't say a word.

The silence that was stretching between them was growing more and more awkward by the second.

Drew looked over at Zach, who shrugged, at a loss for what they could do. He honestly couldn't say what Harriett was thinking, so he didn't know if trying to further argue their case would be a help or a hindrance. Given that Drew—who knew his aunt much better than Zach did—had no clue either, meant he had no hope of figuring it out.

"Aunt Harriett?" Drew finally asked when the silence had gone on for so long that it was almost sentient. "Will you please say something?"

Harriett sighed and leaned forward to place her coffee cup on the table. "I honestly thought it had skipped you like it had skipped your dad and me."

Zach arched a brow. That sounded like . . .

"You already knew about magic?" Drew choked out.

She nodded. "Mom had the gift. At first, she tried to never use it because I think it scared the piss out of her, but when she was stressed or in danger it would just happen. I only saw it a few times myself. From what I've learned since she died, she did master control over it in her later years. I'm guessing that's when she wrote that cookbook of hers. I didn't realise it was a spell book or I wouldn't have given it to you . . . sorry."

"Why didn't you ever tell me about her?" Drew asked, sounding hurt. Zach couldn't really blame him. "You knew Grammy had magic all along and yet you said nothing."

Harriett sighed, and she looked sad. "Because I thought it would be cruel."

"How so?" Zach asked.

She met his gaze, unflinching. "How fair do you think it would be to tell a small boy who had just lost his parents in a horrible car accident that magic is real? How do you think he would have reacted, knowing there are people out there who can do magic, and yet none of them bothered to save his parents? None of them came and used their magic to put food on the table or to turn the hydro back on when I couldn't afford the bills."

Zach inclined his head. "You make a fair point."

"I didn't keep it from you out of spite, love," she told Drew. "If you'd ever shown any inclination then I would have sat you down and told you all about Mom and her abilities, but there was nothing."

Drew took a deep breath and let it out slowly. After a long moment, he nodded. "Okay, I understand your reasons. I guess all of our cards are on the table now."

She gave a wry smile. "Indeed they are. So, you summoned a demon, huh? You always were a terrible cook."

"Hey! I'm not *that* bad!" Drew protested.

"Oh, sweetness," Zach said, leaning over to kiss his cheek. "You have many strengths, but sadly, cooking is *not* one of them."

"Betrayed!" Drew cried, poking out his tongue. "Besides, it's not like you were a *real* demon."

Zach faked-coughed into his hand. *"Beelzebub."*

Turning wide eyes on Zach, Drew held a hand to his heart. "You wound me."

"To be fair, you wound yourself more than I ever could."

"What's that supposed to mean?"

"It means you tripped over your own feet this morning and hit your head on the bathroom cabinet."

"It wasn't my feet!" Drew protested. "I tripped over your catnip toy, thank you very little."

"And why was it out in the first place, hmm?" Zach challenged. "*Maybe* because you were being a little shit and got me high last night so you could have a big laugh."

"Hey! You make it sound like you hated it but you pounced on it as soon as I brought it out."

"Because it smells so damn good," Zach growled.

Drew patted his shoulder. "There, there. If you're struggling with it, there are places and professionals who can help with addiction."

"I don't have an addiction," Zach shot back. "I just have an enabler for a boyfriend."

"Is it so wrong to do things that make you happy?"

"I'm pretty sure it makes you happier."

"Only because you're so cute in your cat form when you're on the nip. Your little bottom sways so much as you stalk across the kitchen."

Harriett snorted. "You two are precious."

They both flinched and turned to look at her. Zach had almost forgotten she was there, and by the guilty look on Drew's face, so had he. "Sorry," Drew told his aunt.

"Don't be. I'm glad to see you've found someone who complements you so well."

"Really?"

She smiled. "Really. Don't get me wrong, I didn't realise quite how big the age gap was between the two of you, but you seem to be making it work."

"We are," Zach assured her, feeling some of his anxiety fade.

"So, Zach, tell me about yourself. What have you been doing since my nephew broke your bonds to that horrible man?"

"Oh, well, I've been keeping busy, especially since Drew has had so many assignments he's had to work on. I've been helping Kensington with a few projects, including writing up a strategy in case there's ever another incursion. I've also been taking some driving lessons," he admitted, and he was amazed at how bashful he felt over that. He rubbed at the back of his neck. "I thought if we had a car we could come and visit you more often. Drew does miss you terribly."

Harriett's eyes softened. "Oh, you are sweet."

"I know, right?" Drew exclaimed. "Can you see why I questioned what sort of demon he could be?"

"You never questioned it," Zach argued.

"Well, maybe not *questioned* it, but I did think you were a really shitty demon."

"You flatter me," Zach drawled, but couldn't help but lean in and give him a soft kiss on the lips.

"You really are very sweet together," Harriett said, then stood up from the armchair. "Right, how about I see about dinner? Then afterward, I have a few things I want to dig out that I think you might find interesting."

The interesting items turned out to be a stack of old notebooks that were bound together by twine. Drew blew a layer of dust off the top of them and then undid the bow which held them together. Zach looked over his shoulder and saw there was loopy handwriting scrawled across the cover of the top book.

The Diary of Winifred E Phillips

1952

"There's a handful of diaries from when she was younger," Harriett explained. "And a couple of other notebooks and stuff. I thought that sorcerer who's training you might be able to tell if they're more spell books or just run-of-the-mill diaries."

"Wow, this is amazing," Drew said as he started to sort through the books. He stopped at one close to the bottom of the pile and began to flip through it.

Zach caught sight of what was written inside and he snatched the book from his hands. "No," he said fiercely. "Absolutely not."

"Why not?" Drew asked with a pout.

Zach held up the book. "This is another cookbook, and not just any cookbook, but it has *cakes* in it."

"And?"

"And it was bad enough when you tried to cook soup. I don't even want to fathom what sort of creature from the beyond you'd summon if you tried to bake a cake!"

Drew huffed. "Honestly, I don't really see the difference."

"And that's why it's so dangerous," Zach told him. "Baking is a very precise art. The measurements need to be exact. It's not like cooking where you can change out ingredients and eyeball how much garlic you're using."

His little shit of a boyfriend actually rolled his eyes at him. "Honestly, Zach. I really think you're overreacting. What could possibly go wrong?"

As Drew looked up from the smashed bowl on his kitchen floor, where flour and egg were mixed in with shards of glass, he decided that next time he got hungry, perhaps he should just eat his words. Picking up *Favourite Cakes and Cookies of Winifred E Phillips,* he held the book out in front of himself as a shield as the zombie advanced on him . . .

Chicken Noodle Soup Recipe

Ingredients:

30 g butter

30 ml olive oil

1 large chopped onion

2 cloves garlic, sliced

225 g carrots, peeled and sliced into chunks

3 stalks celery, sliced into chunks

1 kg boneless, skinless chicken thighs or breasts, cut into chunks

5 cups chicken stock (broth)

2 tsp salt

Black pepper, to taste

1 large lemon, sliced thickly with seeds removed

225 g dried fettuccine or egg noodles, broken into large pieces

Chopped parsley

Freshly grated Parmesan cheese, to taste

Method:

- Put the butter and oil in a large pot over medium heat. When the butter is melted, add the onion, garlic, carrots, and celery. Cook 5 minutes, stirring, or until the onion is softened.

- Add the chicken, stock, 2 teaspoons salt, black pepper, and lemon. Stir. Bring to a simmer, then lower the heat and partially cover the pan. Let the soup bubble gently for 45 minutes. The chicken should be very tender and shred easily with a fork. Remove the lemon slices and discard.

- When the soup is almost done, bring a medium pot of water to the boil. Cook the pasta until al dente, according to package directions. Drain.

- Add the noodles to the soup. Serve warm in bowls, sprinkled with parmesan if desired.

Recipe adapted from one posted by Karen Tedesco on the cooking blog, Family Style Food. It can be found via the following link:
https://familystylefood.com/homemade-chicken-noodle-soup/#wprm-recip e-container-17981

Author Note

T hank you so much for taking the time to read this extended edition of *The Accidental Summoning*. This was my first M/M novel and in the past fifteen months, I've learned so much. Looking back with that newfound knowledge, I made the decision to revamp this book to fix some issues to make it the best version of itself it can be.

First of all, I've removed all of the Harry Potter references from the book. For those in the know, this began as a fanfic I wrote back in 2017 and when I re-wrote it as an original work, I left a lot of the previous references in it. I am ashamed to admit that I kind of live under a rock. I don't watch television and I'm not active in many online spaces. I had heard that Rowling had fallen out of public favour, but I honestly had no idea of the depths of her bigotry until I received a couple of (justifiably) harsh reviews. I then did some research into it and decided to re-write those parts to remove all references to her works. I do apologise for any offence that I may have caused due to that and I aim to be better in the future.

I have also added another chapter as I always felt the book was missing something. It's a short, fun chapter detailing a date Drew and Zach go on.

I feel that it doesn't make the ending feel quite as rushed, and we get to visit Coombs (which I adore).

In this edition, I have also included the short story, *Familiar,* that takes place a year after the events of this book. I do have plans to write a sequel, but I don't have a timeframe for that at the moment. Due to some health issues, my writing speed has drastically reduced and I'm not setting hard deadlines for the near future so as not to disappoint. I encourage you to either join my newsletter or Facebook author group to keep up to date on announcements.

Thank you so much to everyone who has supported me along the way. You have no idea how much I appreciate you. Much love.

Familiar

A Short Story Companion

The House that Zach Bought

The height of summer had passed, but the days were still long and warm. There was a gentle breeze, and Drew Phillips hummed softly to himself as he walked down the wide, tree-lined street. He was walking home after his last class for the week, and he was looking forward to the weekend. Tomorrow was their anniversary, and he had plans. Big plans. But that was tomorrow. He still had several glorious hours of today left, and he planned to make the most of them. Zach would be home soon and they had plans to go for a hike through the Colliery Dam Park before ordering some dinner and then watching a movie.

Drew smiled as he thought of his boyfriend. When they'd first gotten together, they'd discussed what to call one another. He had worried that "boyfriend" was too frivolous to describe his relationship with an eons-old ex-angel. Zach had told him that "partner" made Drew sound ancient, and "lover" sounded like they were in a clandestine relationship that needed to be kept on the down low. In the end, they'd decided that "boyfriend" would make the most sense to everyone else, and so that was the term they used.

Drew was hopeful that from tomorrow they could change the wording to "fiancé."

Was it too cliché to propose on their first anniversary? Probably. Was Drew going to do it anyway? Yes, yes he was. He loved Zach more than he thought possible and he was going to put a ring on it.

Unable to help but feel giddy with excitement, Drew's steps sped up, and he was soon walking up the neat path that led to their small house.

Their house. Drew had a house!

After Zach had been freed from the spell that bound him to the fallen angel, Oberon, Drew had thought his Hellish Amex card would stop working. It didn't. In fact, Zach received a very hefty sum into a bank account from "upper management"—the term he used for the higher angels who ran Heaven like a well-oiled conglomerate. Apparently, it was some sort of severance, recompense, "sorry for abandoning you in Hell for 1400 years" payout. If they'd been human, Drew would have assumed the payout was to bribe Zach into not suing them. Given they were angels, maybe they really did feel bad about what Zach had gone through and wanted to give him the retirement he deserved? Who knew?

Whatever the reason for the payout, Zach had taken it and very quickly spent a good chunk of it. He'd purchased the house—insisting that it be put in both their names—paid for all of Drew's university fees, and then bought Aunt Harriett a small apartment in Victoria. There was still enough left over that he didn't need to work for a living, so he spent his time helping out at the Nightingale Collective and volunteering for several different organisations.

Even if he'd never come clean about his past, there was no way Drew would have continued to believe that Zach was a demon. He was just too damn nice.

He did, however, pass well as a Canadian.

The house was nicer than Drew had ever imagined he'd have. It was located in the university district, in a quiet neighbourhood, and was the first in a row of two-storey townhouses, with a small fenced yard at the front and a garage at the back. It had four bedrooms and three bathrooms. Three! What did people do with three entire bathrooms? Zach had pointed out that one of the bathrooms on the main floor was more of a "powder room" so guests wouldn't have to either use their en suite or go downstairs to use the bathroom there. Drew still thought it was two too many bathrooms for one couple, but it's not like they'd built the house from scratch. He hadn't had a say in how many bathrooms the house came with.

He let himself in through the wooden gate from the road, then crossed the yard to the three steps up to the front porch. He couldn't help but grin as he slid the key into the lock—it was his place. Zach might have paid for it, but he'd made it clear it was theirs, and holy fucking shit, Drew owned a house!

That was never getting old.

The downstairs consisted of two bedrooms, a laundry room that connected to the garage, and a bathroom. One of the bedrooms they had set up as a guest room for when Harriett came to stay with them. Zach had plans to turn the other room into a reading room, but they'd not gotten much further into that project than to buy some flatpack bookcases which were still in their boxes.

Drew toed off his shoes and then climbed the stairs to the upper storey, where he dropped his keys into a bowl that sat on top of a long wooden cabinet. The main living space was a large open-plan area with high ceilings and large windows that let in lots of light. The kitchen at the far end on the right had wooden benchtops and shiny stainless-steel appliances that made Drew feel very grown up. Off the kitchen was a covered balcony that overlooked the park across the road, which made the place feel even more luxurious. Drew had never lived anywhere with a nice view before. It had always been the wall of the building next door, or if he was lucky, a parking lot.

They had turned the second bedroom upstairs into a study of sorts, with desks for both of them. Zach used his desk to work on various projects for Grand Master Bartholomew Kensington, who was the head sorcerer for the Nightingale Collective, and Drew used his space mostly for his university studies, but also his magical studies.

It turned out that Drew came from a long line of witches and he had magic in spades. Kensington had been awed when he'd gotten his first read of Drew's magic, but he'd also been worried about so much raw power in an untrained individual. He had quickly agreed to teach Drew so he didn't inadvertently injure someone, and they met once a week for magical lessons. The house that was used as the Collective's headquarters in Ladysmith wasn't exactly Unseen University, but Drew didn't need a decrepit Tower of Art, a High Energy Magic Building, or a library full of L-space run by an orangutan. As Kensington's only student, his education was catered specifically for him and he didn't need an entire university of indolent and inept old wizards. The one-on-one learning could sometimes be a little overwhelming, but overall Drew was progressing in leaps and bounds.

Glancing at the fancy wrought-iron clock on the wall, Drew saw that he still had almost an hour until Zach would be home, so he headed down to their bedroom. He pulled open the top right-hand drawer of their shared dresser, where he kept his socks, and Drew dug through the pile until his hand found the small ring box. He pulled it out and then went to sit on the end of the bed before he flipped the lid open.

The band inside was simple, and it didn't cost as much as most engagement or wedding rings did. Drew couldn't afford anything pricey, but he'd put a lot of thought into what type of ring would suit Zach, and he was certain this ring was perfect. It was made from black zirconium and had a small ruby inlaid in the centre. The colour combination was reminiscent of Zach's beautiful wings. It was elegant and stylish, just like Zach himself, and the metal had been subjected to extreme temperatures and yet emerged transformed into something truly beautiful.

Just like Zach.

Drew knew his inexperience with relationships made him uncertain at times, but in this he was positive he had made the right choice. He couldn't wait to get down on one knee and offer Zach this ring in exchange for forever with him. Marriage wasn't for everyone, and Drew had honestly never thought he'd ever want to get married, but for some reason, it felt right to him now.

He heard the front door close and jerked in surprise. "Hey, sweetness. I'm home!" Zach's voice drifted up the stairs.

Drew swore and snapped the box shut, then quickly shoved it back into the drawer, burying it under his socks. He hurried down the short hallway into the living area just as Zach appeared at the top of the stairs. He was looking gorgeous as usual, his dark hair perfectly styled, his golden whiskey-coloured eyes bright, and his tall frame draped in a tailored shirt and suit pants that clung to every muscle. His wings were hidden, but Drew knew they could appear at a moment's notice whenever Zach wished. "Hey," he said with a big smile, crossing to Zach and tilting his head up for a kiss.

"Hey," Zach murmured against his lips.

"You're back early," Drew noted.

"Yeah. Kensington and Simon got called off to some sort of disaster somewhere, so I figured I'd call it a day."

Drew frowned. "Is everything alright?"

Zach shrugged. "They didn't look too stressed, so I don't think it's apocalyptic or anything."

Rolling his eyes, Drew said, "As long as the world isn't ending, I guess we're not supposed to be concerned."

"There wasn't a supercell full of harpies hovering over the island, and I haven't seen any hobbits with an unhinged, anemic stalker trekking over to Mt Baker to destroy a ring, so I think it's okay," Zach assured him. "Besides, if the shit really hits the fan, they'll call us in for backup."

"I'm not complaining that they haven't. I am totally on board with not having to be on call for end-of-times catastrophes. I'm very happy to leave that up to the experts at the Collective. One big disaster a year is enough for me, thank you very much." And it was true. Drew may have discovered he'd inherited a strong magical ability, but no matter how much Kensington hinted that Drew was perfectly suited to join the Nightingale Collective, he wasn't particularly interested.

Not yet at least.

Sure, in ten or twenty years he might consider it, but for now he wanted to keep his life as normal as possible. He'd finish his degree, find a job, and live life as an everyday Joe. Kind of. As much as one could when they were dating—and would hopefully be engaged to—an ex-angel, had magical lessons once a week, and knew about the existence of the paranormal.

Drew didn't have heroic aspirations. He didn't want to be the one who rode in at the last moment and saved the day. He just wanted a simple life. Drew knew that the cards he'd been dealt meant his life wouldn't truly be simple, but he could mitigate the craziness to some degree, couldn't he?

Fuck, he really hoped he could.

"Did you still want to go for a walk?" Zach asked.

"If you don't mind."

Zach smiled and bent down once again to give him a kiss. "Not at all. I just needed to know if I was changing into hiking clothes or pyjamas."

Drew grinned. "Hiking clothes now, pyjamas later, and if you're really good, nothing at all after that."

Smirking, Zach crossed to the walk-in wardrobe, unbuttoning his shirt as he went. "I shall do my utter best to behave."

Fight of the Feathers

There was nothing that Zachariel liked more than seeing Drew happy and content. The sunlight trickled down through the dense canopy of trees above them, making it seem like the freckles painted across his nose and cheeks were dancing. His pale blue eyes were almost dreamy beneath his mop of brown hair, and each time he looked over at Zach, he'd give him a sweet smile. He was absolutely stunning.

He was also absolutely clumsy. Tripping over a tree root that crossed the path, Drew tumbled to the ground, hitting it with a loud "oof."

"Shit, are you okay?" Zach asked, hurrying over and pulling him to his feet.

"I think so," Drew said.

Wanting to be sure, Zach began checking him over for injuries. He took Drew's hands in his, checking his palms for scrapes and grazes before moving on. He winced as he saw the blood trickling down from the scratch on his knee and led Drew over to a tree stump so he could clean him up.

"Zach, I'm fine," Drew assured him.

"You're bleeding," Zach argued, crouching down as he pulled a pack of wet wipes from his pocket along with a Band-Aid. He'd taken to carrying a few first-aid supplies whenever they went for a hike because it was inevitable that Drew would trip, stumble, or injure himself in some way each time.

"Not enough to require a transfusion," he said, rolling his eyes. "It's already stopped bleeding."

"Just shush and let me fuss." Zach gently cleaned the cut with a wipe and then blew on it to dry the skin. He looked up to see Drew looking at him with half fondness and half exasperation. "What?"

"Nothing. I just love you, is all."

Zach's heart thumped against his rib cage. After all he'd endured, he had never even dreamed he would one day be this happy. He felt his eyes crinkle as he smiled dopily up at him. "Love you too, sweetness." He peeled the backing off the Band-Aid and covered the scratch with it, smoothing the edges to make sure it was sticking to the skin. Then he dropped a kiss to the top of it and stood up from his crouch. He held his hand out to Drew. "Shall we?"

Drew took his hand and allowed himself to be pulled to his feet, but before they could take a single step, there came the sound of furious flapping and then Drew was obscured by a wall of black feathers.

Zach's own wings snapped out at the threat and he lunged forward to protect Drew, only to be forced back by a vicious assault from beak and feathers. What the hell was this creature? It appeared to be slightly bigger than a crow or raven, but that was all Zach could determine as he warded off a brutal beak and sharp claws.

"Zach!" Drew cried. "What the hell is happening?"

"I don't know!" Zach bit out, hissing as he felt a claw rip the skin open on his forearm.

The bird flapped its wings once more, all of its ire seemingly directed towards Zach, and he caught sight of an eye blacker than the inside of the

Devil's ass. Then it was using its perch on Drew's shoulder as a springboard and it launched itself at Zach, clawing and slashing. It was tiny but feral, and Zach was definitely losing this battle. The thing was too fast for him to catch, and all he could do was defend against the unprovoked attack.

"Enough!" Drew's voice cut through the chaos, leaving only silence and stillness in its wake. Zach's ears popped at the strength of the magic behind Drew's command, but he, like their feathered attacker, was frozen to the spot.

Drew stepped around the feathery explosion that was hanging in the air like some sort of stupidly expensive, impractical lamp shade. As soon as his hands touched Zach's face, the spell was broken and Zach could move. He pulled Drew into his arms, his own wings surrounding them in a protective circle. They were both breathing hard, and Zach's face and arms stung from numerous wounds.

"What the actual fuck was that?" Drew asked, pressing his face against Zach's chest.

"I'm not sure," Zach admitted.

"Do you think it was sent from Hell?"

"Possibly, but in all the commotion I didn't get a good look at it."

Drew raised his head and then turned in Zach's arms. "Let's figure out what it is."

Reluctantly letting his wings fold back against his back, Zach stepped towards the creature. Its wings were a blur, frozen as they were mid-flight. He and Drew circled to the left and finally caught an unimpeded view of the creature for the first time.

"Is that . . . is that a chicken?" Drew exclaimed.

Zach furrowed his brows as he inspected the bird. "It kind of looks like one, I guess."

Drew whipped out his phone and took a photo of the bird. He then did a Lens search before grunting in surprise. "According to Google, it's an Ayam Cemani. A hen, I'm guessing?"

Zach looked from the results page to the chicken, noting the glossy black feathers, small black comb, and beady black eyes. The chicken may have been frozen, but it was still cognizant and Zach could see the malice in those eyes. "It does look like one."

"It says these come from Java and are really uncommon. What the hell is a rare breed of chicken doing wandering around Collier Dam Park?" Drew mused.

"More to the point, why is it attacking us?" Zach asked.

"You," Drew corrected. "It was attacking you. It didn't seem fazed by me. I wonder what it's doing here?"

Zach held up his torn and bloody arms and gave a feral smile. "Hell's version of Uber Eats?" he suggested.

Quick as a whip, Drew snatched the hen from the air and cradled her in his arms. "You are not eating her!" he cried. The chicken, which had unfrozen as soon as Drew had touched her, *bokked* angrily at Zach.

"Why not? She tried to eat me!"

"She's tiny! She wasn't a threat to you," Drew chastised.

"Exhibit A!" Zach exclaimed, shaking his wounded arms in Drew's face to make his point.

"Don't be such a baby," Drew chided. "She was just scared." He nuzzled against the hen's feathered neck. "Weren't you, girl? You were just scared," he said in a cutesy voice. "Let's get you home, get you something to eat, and see if we can find your owner on any lost pet pages."

"Wait, what?" Zach frowned. "Why are we taking that thing home with us?"

"Because she's probably a missing pet and someone might be looking for her," Drew explained patiently, as if Zach was a little bit daft. "Besides, I don't want her becoming cougar food."

"She's more than capable of defending herself," Zach argued. He held out his arms once more, a little annoyed that Drew wasn't taking his wounds more seriously. Zach had patched up his wounds, after all. "Once again . . . Exhibit A."

"You're just grumpy that you were beaten in a fight by a three-pound hen."

Trying not to pout, Zach muttered, "Am not."

Drew leaned in and gave him a kiss. "Come on, you sore loser. Let's head home. The sooner we find her owners, the sooner you can go back to being the biggest baddest winged creature in town." Then he turned around and started walking back the way they'd come, towards home.

Over his shoulder, Zach saw the hen give him a smug look before she settled down and snuggled against Drew's chest.

Eyes narrowed, Zach stalked after them.

"I can't believe no one is missing such a sweet girl," Drew said, looking up from his laptop.

Zach grunted. "You didn't find any 'missing demon chicken' posts on Facebook, then?"

"Maybe I'm looking in the wrong groups," Drew drawled. "Perhaps you could look in your old groups for actual demons that are missing a pet chicken."

The chicken—who was sitting on top of Zach's favourite cushion on the sofa next to Drew—gave Zach a triumphant look and then began to preen the feathers on her chest. Drew absently reached down and began to stroke along her back, and much to Zach's astonishment, the hen not only allowed the petting but seemed to enjoy it. He glared at her, feeling strangely jealous of the attention she was getting from his boyfriend.

A few minutes later, Drew made a humming noise.

"Find something?" Zach asked.

"No, still nothing. It looks like we'll need to set her up a perch and buy some specialised grain mix, as well as a waterer, but I guess a small container will do for now."

"Excuse me?" Zach couldn't possibly have heard that right.

"I mean, if we don't find her owners, we'll need to build her a pen outside, but I'm thinking for now she'll be okay inside. We'll just need to keep her away from the bedrooms that have carpet."

"We are not keeping a chicken inside!" Zach protested.

"Why not?" Drew asked, frowning.

"Because . . . because it's a chicken!" Zach sputtered.

Drew's eyes narrowed. "And? She's scared and alone and I'm not just dumping her back in the woods to be eaten by some predator!"

"I'm pretty sure she could take on the *actual* Predator and come out victorious."

"She's tiny! She'll become something's lunch."

"Yeah, mine if I have my way!"

"Zach!"

He gave his boyfriend a serious look, but he could already tell that he'd lost this fight. "Drew."

"Please, will you help me look after her?" Drew asked, his eyes wide and imploring.

Zach threw his arms up in the air. "Fine! What is it that we need?"

Welcome to the Family

The house was quiet. Zach had gone to Home Depot to buy supplies, leaving Drew and the chicken alone. He'd laid some newspaper down in the corner, along with a bowl of water, and she'd already had a long drink, dipping her beak into the bowl over and over until she'd sated her thirst. She'd also relieved herself, twice, both times keeping it to the newspaper. In fact, it was the second time, when she'd gotten down off the couch, walked over to the corner to shit, and then returned to the couch that sent alarm bells ringing.

Unless she was a highly trained indoor pet—which wasn't outside the realm of possibility, but highly unlikely—she might not be a regular, run-of-the-mill chicken. Drew snapped a photo of her and sent a text off to Kensington, asking him to drop around when he was finished with his emergency.

"What exactly are you?" Drew mused as he stroked the soft feathers on her back. He couldn't believe how inky black her colouring was. Zach's wing feathers were black, but they shone with a tinge of red. These feathers were so dark it was as if they sucked all the light into them like a singularity. Her black skin, eyes, and comb were initially unnerving, but the more she sat calmly next to Drew and allowed him to pet her, the more he found her beautiful.

"I just have a feeling you're not someone's lost pet," he murmured to her.

The chicken made a soft trilling noise that almost sounded like a purr.

"I think you might end up living here with us. Would you like that?"

Another chicken-like purr.

"You'd have to be nicer to Zach, though. You really did a number on his arm and that's not okay. He takes good care of me, so I won't have you hurting him. Okay?"

The hen blinked slowly in his direction.

Drew had the crazy idea that she could understand every word he was saying to her. But was it really so crazy? Zach could transform into a freaking cat, and when he was in that form they communicated telepathically with one another. Was an intelligent chicken so impossible?

"I guess we'll need to give you a name if you're going to stay here with us," Drew told her. "How about Ebony?"

The hen gave him a haughty glare.

"Hmmm, what about Sabrina?"

She *bokked* grumpily.

"Raven?"

She nipped at his finger.

"Ow!" Drew sucked his finger into his mouth. "Fine, we won't use any of those. What the hell do you want to be called then?"

Leila.

The thought came to him with such clarity that Drew gave the hen a shrewd look. Had that idea come from him or from her? "If you can understand me, *bok* once for yes and twice for no."

Leila stayed silent, but she did give him a look reminiscent of the ones that Harriett used when Drew had done something particularly stupid. Before Drew could come up with other ways to test her sentience, he heard the door to the garage open and close and then voices on the stairs. A moment later Zach appeared, carrying a plank of two-by-four timber, and Kensington followed him in, laden down with a plastic feeder, waterer, and a bag of feed.

"Hey," Drew said, jumping to his feet and coming over to unload his mentor's arms. "Thanks so much for coming."

Kensington didn't reply, too busy staring at Leila.

"What is it?" Drew asked.

"That is not a normal chicken," Kensington said slowly.

"I fucking knew it!" Zach crowed. "She's a demon chicken, isn't she?!"

Kensington shot him a withering glance. "Of course not. Don't be ridiculous."

Zach held up his arms, where his numerous wounds were starting to scab over, and waved them around. "Why is the court dismissing the evidence presented in Exhibit A?" he demanded.

"Drew," Kensington said as they both ignored Zach's dramatics. "You seem to have gotten yourself a familiar."

"Excuse me?" Drew asked, shocked.

"I've never heard of familiars outside of fairy tales," Zach said.

"They're something that only the most powerful of magic users have," Kensington explained. "They're not just for witches, but sorcerers, wizards, and warlocks too. We don't know where they come from, but we do know that the familiar chooses the magic user and not the other way round. To be honest, Drew, your power is so great that I'm not at all surprised to find you've acquired a familiar."

"Leila. Her name is Leila," Drew told them.

"It's a pleasure to make your acquaintance, Laila," the Grand Master told the hen formally, adding a little bow at the end. Leila ducked her head in a return bow.

Zach groaned. "So, I guess we're keeping the chicken?"

Drew grinned. "We're keeping the chicken."

Glaring at Leila, Zach pointed two fingers at his eyes and then turned them to point at her. "I'm watching you, chicken."

Leila just did her little chirrup-purr thing and ignored him.

And just like that, Drew's life changed once more.

About the author

Addison Acres has a big smile and a gentle temperament, which leads many to believe that she is sweet and innocent. Given that she loves to write raunchy stories, many with a hefty dash of kink and taboo, this is patently untrue.

Addison lives in the Wheatbelt of Western Australia, swears like a pirate, and is a profound supporter of the Oxford comma. She is a proud pansexual and strident advocate for LGBTQIA+ rights.

Come join her Facebook group, Addison's Addicts, or for a complete list of her works, visit her website https://addisonacresauthor.mailerpage.io/. You can also subscribe to her newsletter for freebies, news, and her general ramblings.

Scan the QR code to visit her Amazon or Smashword stores.